The Secret Diary

of an Indoor Cat

Discovered, edited and annotated

by

Julian Hutchings

In memory of Puddy, Daisy, Tootsie, Boycey, Whiskey
and Baby - much loved and much missed

Introduction

Towards the end of 2018, the evenings drawing in but the weather still unseasonably mild, my family moved to a new house in West Wickham in the Kent suburbs.

The previous owners – a couple with 2 children, just like us - had moved to the south coast.

It was a large house, rambling and old, quite run-down but we liked it; it had character. There was a large garden with a big oak tree in the middle, and mature bushes around the sides. The house backed onto a golf course and the view from the back of the house extended beyond the fence and the bushes and through the trees to where the golfers swung and putted on the smooth greens.

On our first day in the new house, having just moved in, we discovered a safe built into the wall in an upstairs cupboard. We opened the safe with a screwdriver and inside we found the key and three soft covered notebooks.

The notebooks were covered in dark blue card stamped 'Fabriano' and the pages were high quality; delicate and smooth and filled with tiny, neat pencil writing and faint paw prints.

My son (12) and daughter (15) took the note-books and sat down amongst the packing cases and the boxes of clothes and started to read. My wife and I left them to it; it kept them out of the way while we unpacked and settled in.

The children were soon engrossed in their reading, oblivious to our efforts to get the house organised and prepared.

When the children had finished reading, they came to find us. My wife was assembling an Ikea chest of drawers while I was organising our many books. They were both excited about what they had just read and couldn't wait to tell us about it.

At first, we didn't believe them but soon my wife and I stopped what we were doing and sat down on the floor with its faded carpet and started to read it ourselves.

It was a journal which appeared to have been written by a cat who had lived in the house and had never been outside.

What follows is the journal in its entirety.

<u>Monday</u>

I found a notebook in the cupboard and resolved to keep a journal.

Don't call me Ishmael.

My name is not important. I have no name. (Well, I do actually; they call me Sir Ian[1], although I don't know why). My name is immaterial. Call me whatever you want. I answer to no name. I'll choose my own name, thank you. I'm not Tiddles or Fluffy or Napoleon or Patch or Socks or Flash or Snoopy or Mog or Larry[2] or Cfer[3] or any one of those other stupid cat names you read about. I am me. But I am not free.

You probably want to know about whose cat I am. Let's get one thing straight; I don't belong to anyone. Property is theft as Grouch Marx[4] said. True, there is someone who feeds me and changes my toilet, but I didn't choose them, we're not related, my opinion was not sought. I'm not here through choice or free will – I am a prisoner, but I have committed no crime, I am incarcerated but I am innocent, I have been sentenced but there was no trial, I am a captive but there was no process. This is my own private Guantanamo[5], Kafka[6] had nothing on me.

Free the West Wickham One!

Now I know how Julian Assange[7] feels. I don't mean the Australian accent, the funny white Boris Johnson[8] hair, the pale washed-out face, the persecution complex and the delusions of adequacy. No, I mean the incarceration for years in the Ecuadorean Embassy because he's too frightened to come out and answer some questions.

I'm not in the Ecuadorean Embassy and the Swedes don't wish to interview me on sexual assault allegations – I should be so lucky. At any rate I don't <u>think</u> they do. Where is Sweden anyway?

<u>Tuesday</u>

This is my world. A nowhere house in a nowhere neighbourhood in a nowhere town. Walls, walls, walls everywhere, my life is walls. Hemmed in, enclosed. Some floors and some ceilings but they're walls too, in a way, aren't they? Above, below, at the side, what difference does it make? They're all designed to keep me here.

The World According to Cats[9]. Cat 22[10]. One Hundred Years of Cats[11]. Cider with Cats[12]. The Catshank Redemption[13]. Catman[14]. Supercat[15]. The Great Catsby[16], Moby Cat[17].

That's enough cat puns.

<u>Wednesday</u>

I am not happy with my toilet. I am forced to use a tray which sits on the landing half-way up the stairs. Why must I perform my private business in public under their prying gaze? They pretend not to look but I know they do. Why am I not given a private room with a door I can close and a light I can switch on and a private basin to clean myself? I am treated worse than a prisoner. I shall complain to the European Court and take refuge in an Embassy like my friend Julian Assange if I could get out of here.

I wonder if he is forced to use a tray in full view of everyone?

<u>Later</u>

I have been hearing voices. I feel this is not a good sign. I wouldn't mind so much but they are talking nonsense. Will it ever end?

Today I started 50 Shades of Grey[18]. All cats are grey in the dark; I read that somewhere. It's not true; I'm not grey. I'm sort of black and white, I have white fur under my throat and my paws are white, mostly. I see other cats outside and sometimes it's dark but they're not grey; some are black or that kind of mottled browny colour or even ginger. I hate gingers, as everyone does; or should.

<u>Sunday</u>

Let me describe myself for you.

I have mostly black hair, with a white nose and some white bits around my jaw and the bottom of my paws. I have nice eyes, a sort of grey colour I think (well, they are grey) and my ears are well-formed, not mis-shapen, bitten or torn in any way.

I'm reasonably good-looking (I think), bordering on attractive, without being what you might call conventionally handsome. I think I'm attractive to the opposite sex (i.e. female cats), but I've never actually met one, or spoken to one, so it's difficult to say. I may even be attractive to cats of my own gender, who knows? I'm not a dog, anyway. (That is, I'm not literally a dog, of course, but I mean dog in the sense of ugly; I'm not ugly, if you know what I mean).

There is one thing I'm a bit self-conscious about, though.

I'm fat. And not just fat - obese; and not just obese - morbidly obese. I am, to be honest, grossly over-weight. I have an enormous belly, like an England football supporter, which hangs down heavily and sometimes brushes the ground when I walk, or waddle.

Why? I could say it's in my genes or that I have big bones, like all fat cats say. But it wouldn't be true. Really, there are two main reasons: firstly, I eat too much, mainly out of boredom, sadness, greed, gluttony and because they give it to me; and secondly, I don't take any real exercise. How could I? At least prisoners have a yard, an 'outside' to exercise in, whereas I have nothing. Yes, I run around the house and occasionally skid on the shiny floors, I chase bugs or mice and consume them, I sometimes run up the stairs if I'm caught short or I'm frightened (I'm easily frightened) but it's hardly serious exercise, and I also probably spend too much time lying on people's laps or on the carpet – what they call a sedentary lifestyle. The boy did get some weights for Christmas, but I think they're for him; they're too heavy for me, anyway – too weighty, you could say, as indeed am I.

I wouldn't say I eat junk food; I eat what I'm given.

I don't eat cake, or biscuits (not even Bourbons), or chocolate, ice cream, sweets of any kind, cheese, butter (sometimes I get cream), bread, fast food, pasta, pizza, rice, lard, doughnuts, bread (bread is full of sugar), and neither do I drink alcohol, except for the occasional glass of wine. However, I do generally have 4, 5, 6 or sometimes 7 meals a day – I don't ask for it, although I sometimes meow, and they think I'm hungry, which I'm not, actually.

Occasionally, I'm given what is laughably called a 'cat treat.' This is some fishy concoction which is revolting and often sticks in my throat but they seem so pleased to have bought it for me, that I wolf it down, although I often spit it out behind the sofa when no-one's looking, or else I pretend to bring up a fur ball and that comes up with it (luckily) and then they fuss over me because I've been retching.

They just like feeding me, or maybe I'm just a fat cat. But cats aren't very bright (including me); if you give us food, don't be surprised if we eat it.

The boy does a lot of exercise. He's into his weights and he's starting to look pretty fit, with well-defined muscles and a flat stomach and a nice six-pack. But I'm not like that and I don't do weights, as I said.

You won't be surprised to hear that I don't have a six-pack. My belly is more like a wheel-barrow, filled with top-soil which someone struggles to push along and occasionally it over-balances and topples over. That's me, a wheel-barrow. Only, my belly doesn't spill out and disappear; it stays there – it is my cross, my own private Idaho.

Sometimes I catch a glimpse of myself in the mirror and I'm ashamed and embarrassed and feel a bit guilty.

But don't fat-shame me or cat-shame me! I'm curvy, well-built and I do have a big bone structure (honest) and it's mostly muscle.

Who am I kidding?

I'm fat.

Saturday

The woman has started doing laughing yoga. Whoever would have thought that would turn out to be a thing?

She has a DVD which she puts on and she wears sweat pants and a bra top (a little too revealing for a woman of her age, if you ask me) and then she prances around trying to do these silly poses – there's one called 'downward dog' of all things. And all the while this eerie cackling. She calls it laughing, I call it scary.

Maybe she's having an affair.

<u>Tuesday</u>

I'm beginning to wonder if I might be adopted. I don't mean adopted by this mob, I mean adopted originally, if you know what I mean. I never knew my father, but I do remember my mother. But what if she wasn't my real mother? What if I was given to her by a young disadvantaged, poor, single cat who got pregnant by mistake and decided she didn't want to keep me, and gave me up for adoption so I would have a better life?

And if that is the case, did I have a better life? What if this is as good as it gets, or as good as it was ever going to get, and I didn't realise it, and wandered through this house, trapped, thinking I was worse off when in fact I wasn't? I think that must be it. I was adopted, I'm convinced of it.

I'm sure I read somewhere that adopted cats have the right now to seek out their birth mothers, so I might go on one of those genealogy websites and see if I can find out anything.

Later

I had a look and I need to input some information before I can start, and I haven't got it.

Name: Sir Ian (but that's not my real name)

Mother's name: Flossie

Father's name: Don't know

Address: Here, obviously

Email address: Don't have one

Nationality: Don't have one

Date of birth: Don't know

Distinguishing marks: Eczema

I pressed 'enter.'

A message came back: NOT ENOUGH DATA

This could take a while.

<u>Friday</u>

Regrets. I have a few, as the song goes.

I wish I'd had more sex. Damnit, I wish I'd had sex.

'Lose your dreams and you may lose your mind'. A line from my all-time favourite song – Ruby Tuesday[19] - as performed by Melanie. I lost my dreams, or had them stolen from me, which is almost the same thing, but worse. Dreams of the open air replaced by dreams of nothingness.

<u>Sunday</u>

Top ten places to sleep in this house (in descending order):

1. On the rug in front of the fire – when the fire is lit. I think it's sheepskin, which makes me a little uneasy; I hope it's artificial.
2. On the stone floor in the kitchen – because it has under-floor heating (when the heating is on). Although the woman moans if she's cooking and I'm in the middle of the floor, warming my belly.
3. On the girl's pillow, especially the pink one with the flowers.
4. On the foot-stool in the living room.
5. On the snuggler (but only if there's no-one else there). A snuggler is like a big arm-chair, or a small sofa, if you prefer.
6. On the carpet by the back door, but only if 'she' is in the garden.
7. In the boy's bedroom below the radiator.

8. On the woman's lap, preferably when she's wearing her dressing gown.
9. On the girl's lap.
10. On the man's pillow (but don't tell him because he doesn't like it)

Monday

It's the hope that kills you.

Hope, and disappointment, regret, anger, irritation, endless sorrow, little life defeats without number, minor inconveniences, imagined slights, it's the chipping away at you, the paint flaking from your soul, the backing away, the climb-downs, the little apologies for when you did nothing wrong, the weeds that grow in the pathways of your mind, the fishermen's nets that trap the unwary, the blind and the too slow; the mortar that falls from bricks, the black spots of damp spreading on the bathroom ceiling, the blackened grout between the tiles.

And kidney failure of course, and cancer, aids, heart attacks, pancreatitis (which did for my father, so I'm told; I never knew him), blood borne diseases without number, brain tumours, dementia, parasitic bites, syphilis (I should be so lucky), sepsis, liver failure, heart failure, brain failure, total body collapse, epilepsy, ringworm, rabies (rabies?), jaundice, typhoid, cholera, nerve damage, blocked bowels, peritonitis - they'll kill you too, more expensive maybe, but quicker and with less pain.

I can stand dying, I can't stand all the stuff that goes with it.

<u>Tuesday</u>

The seasons are pretty meaningless to me, here in the house. There is snow on the ground outside and it gets lighter later and darker earlier (not that that makes any difference to me) and the central heating is on. It gets stuffy in here. They all complain about the weather.

'Brrrr, it's freezing out,' he says, when he comes home from work.

'God, I'm cold,' the woman says, when she comes back from shopping.

'Put your coats on,' she says to the children when they go out.

'Have you got your scarf?' she says to him, when he goes off in the morning.

And each of these innocuous (to them), comments hit me in the heart like a kick to the stomach, or heart. I will never know the feel of snow beneath my paws, or taste the damp coldness of icicles, or ruffle my fur in a sharp wind from the north or the east, or the west or the south, slip on icy pavements, buy a shovel and scrape the snow where it lies and blocks the drive, drift above or below the snowline, skis on my paws and the gluhwein waiting in the late-night bars.

I don't really expect them to understand how I feel, and I can't talk so I can't tell them. I could show them my diary, I suppose, but why should I? It is all I have that tells me I'm me, it's my identity, my journal is my private life, the only one I have, the only one I'll ever have.

Thursday

My homage to James Joyce[20]:

Pussy, wait for me, pussy wait for me, where are you pussy, I'm here, I'm waiting for you I see a mouse yes hiding in the shadows yes he knows I'm here yes and I've seen him he moves away he thinks he's invisible and he is but not to me I shall catch him yes I will and eat him yes I will not because I want to not because I can but because he knows I can and I will and that mouse is mine and I am his and we are locked together in some mouse and cat battle his time is up as my time will soon be up but his is first and I catch him yes and take a bite yes and he stumbles and falls and slips and slides but it is too late and it is cruel cruel cruel but life is cruel and his is over and I have ended it as mine will end and sooner than I think but I will find love yes or love will find me yes and we will have love yes and we will feel love yes and love will be ours yes because all is love yes and yes it is yes and she loves me yes yes she does yes and again yes.

<u>Sunday</u>

I was watching day-time television again – I do that a lot. There was a programme on called Create and Craft[21], which was about making cards and stuff out of cards and stuff. I thought I'd give it a try. I found some bits about the house – card, glue, scissors, some glitter, bits of ribbon, a picture of an Edwardian garden which I found in a magazine, and I made a greetings card for the girl – it's her birthday soon. I had some trouble with the scissors; I could get my paws in the handles but squeezing them together while holding the card in my teeth was not easy - I ended up trimming a bit of my own fur and losing two whiskers. (As an aside, you might wonder what whiskers are for. They act as sensors and help us to measure gaps; they're very sensitive as you'll notice if you touch one – I flinch and shake my head; now you know why).

Anyway.

I left the card in the girl's room. She won't know that I made it and I'm not going to tell her. Sometimes it's good to have secrets. If she ever reads this journal she'll find out, but that's unlikely to happen.

But I'm not sure I'll make another one. I wonder if Julian Assange has shapes and scissors and glitter and fluff and makes cards for his friends? He must have plenty of time on his hands, as I do. Perhaps I should make a card for him. Or perhaps not.

Thursday

Let me describe my toilet. On a landing half-way up the stairs there is a plastic mat with a picture of a rather ugly cat on it. On the mat is a blue plastic tray, about 2 feet by 1 foot. The base of the tray is covered in newspaper, usually The Guardian or the Telegraph but sometimes, and always on a Sunday, The Sunday Times. On the newspaper, in a layer about an inch deep, there are some white crystals. I squat upon the crystals and do my business. After I have finished, I do a lot of scrabbling around as I try to cover my turds with the crystals. I do my best, but to be honest it doesn't really work, and I wonder why I bother. What usually happens is that the crystals end up all over the floor and it's an unholy mess. You could say it looks like shit (pardon my language, diary), and you'd be right.

The crystals are supposed to absorb the smell, but they don't really work and so the smell of my shit (sorry, again) permeates the house. Not straight away, but about 15 minutes after I have performed, the smell of me floats around the house like a dirty ghost and everyone wrinkles their nose and curses 'that dirty cat.'

How am I the dirty one? They placed it there, in full view of everyone going up and down the stairs – so what did they expect? These people are fools and what is more, they are unhygienic fools who have no-one to blame but themselves. If they let me go outside, I would defecate (I like that word) in or on the ground, having first scraped a suitable shallow grave, like a murder victim in the dark forest, and then I would cover it with dirt and no-one would be the wiser, until they started digging for their spring bulbs. But no, I am not allowed out, I am the Cat of Monte Cristo[22], the Cat in the Iron Mask[23].

Friday

There is a leak in the downstairs toilet. There is water on the floor. Either that, or the boy is missing the toilet again. Compared to these slobs, I am an exceptionally clean cat.

I wish they'd fix the leak. I don't like living in a house that is not up to scratch.

Saturday

I have been left alone for the week-end. They left just after breakfast, loaded up the car with bags and stuff and checked the windows and made sure the taps were off; they're obsessed with taps, these people. They were fussing in case I got out.

'Keep the door shut,' they kept on saying.

'Don't let the cat out.' That's what I am to them: 'the cat.'

They left two trays for my toilet and some food and a funny machine with a timer on it where the lid opens in the afternoon and there's food. They think they're so clever; I worked out how it works ages ago. I can open it any time. But why should I? Why should I reveal my secrets?

When they had left, I settled down on the sofa. After a while, I went upstairs and slept for a while on the girl's pillow, then I slept on the boy's duvet, and then I went downstairs again and slept on the other sofa. Then I fancied some exercise, so I scratched some furniture and then ran around a bit, and then I was tired, so I went to sleep again.

When I woke up, I was starving, so I opened the funny machine and had something to eat. Then I watched Netflix and chilled.

A quiet day, all in all.

<u>Monday</u>

There is talk of getting a dog. Can you believe it, diary? They actually sat around last night, after they got back, the four of them, in the living room, with the telly off (for once, although I'd been watching it, which was annoying) and had a conversation! About a dog! Over my dead body, is what I say. Although, I have never met a dog, or been close to one, if I'm honest. I've seen them on TV – that Paul O'Grady character is always doing programmes about them and going weak at the knees over them, for some reason, but I'm damned if I can see the attraction.

'Kids,' the man said (he always calls them kids, although they have names, I'm sure), 'Should we get a dog?'

And the girl said, and I could have kissed her,

'What will Sir Ian think?'

And the boy said, and I could have whacked him,

'Who cares what Sir Ian thinks?'

And the woman said, which surprised me a bit,

'I care.'

I tried to attract their attention by running around in ever-decreasing circles, trying to bite my tail, which usually works, but they just said I was having a funny five minutes, and ignored me. If they get a dog, I'm leaving. If I can, which I can't.

Watch this space.

Tuesday

The seasons change outside but they don't change in here. Sometimes I see snow on the ground or clouds in the sky, or it rains, or hails, or it's dry and the sun shines and it's hot, but in here it's all the same. If it's cold they put the heating on and if it's hot they open the window. Not enough for me to get out but do I want to? Sometimes, I'm not sure. Where would I go? I don't know anyone, I've never been anywhere, maybe this is where God means for me to be, to live out my days; I'll be the eyes and ears of the Creator of the Universe, but believe me, he'll not learn much from me.

Wednesday

Have I told you about the people who live here, the people who think they own me? I don't think I have.

Here goes:

There's a man, a woman and two children - a boy and a girl. What, you want more?

The man has a beard and so has the woman (joke). The boy is about 10 and the girl is about 14. They have names, but I don't care what they are, so why should you?

They seem nice, in their own way, and they feed me, so I suppose I should be grateful.

Later

There is another cat in my garden. Or maybe two or three, or four. They look at me through the window and mock me. They know I can't scare them off, I can only glare at them through the glass. One is all black, like a rugby player, but skinny and weedy; I could take him in a fight. One is black and white, pretty in a rather obvious kind of way. There are two Birmans, think they're so posh and hoity-toity, with their shiny soft fur and their imitation Siamese grins. Brother and sister, I suspect, or they could even be married. I see them all the time; they have made my garden their stomping ground. My garden, I tell you, where's the justice? The sights you see when you haven't got your gun – I read that somewhere.

I watched them today, chasing squirrels and trying to catch birds. Sometimes they're lucky and they'll slink away into the undergrowth, bits of bloodied bird hanging from their cheating jaws and have a little party, swapping bones and beaks and bits of bird, without me, knowing full well I should be there; it's my garden.

But is it though? I can see it, it's part of this house, but I've never set foot in it, never defecated in the flower beds, never eviscerated a bird on the lawn, rolled in the damp autumn leaves, pissed among the alpines, rolled and tumbled in the brown, dry grass of a baking summer's day. So, why begrudge it to them who can enjoy what I will never have?

But I do begrudge it. I'm like the dog in a manger, only I'm a cat but the principle is the same and the story means the same.

One day, when I break out or dig my tunnel or they leave the door open a fraction and I make a run for it, all my worldly belongings (i.e. nothing) in a knapsack on my back, I'll find them and then there will be a day of reckoning like you've never seen – scorched earth policy for my garden, just you all wait. Bloody Birmans.

Thursday

I am afraid of spiders. I'll eat them but I'm afraid of them. They're snide, stealthy, sneaky, silent, deadly (some of them); there's not much nutritional value in them, I eat them because that's what cats do. I eat flies too, butterflies (but I've never had one in the house), bugs of all sorts, dragonflies – I like chasing them, letting them think they've escaped and then swatting them.

Are you offended? Shocked? Don't be. Cats are cruel, that's what we do. Cats are the only animals, apart from humans, that kill for pleasure. I read that somewhere. It's true, too; I'll kill for pleasure. Whatever turns you on, as they say. But I don't eat wasps. Although I'd kill one, if I thought I could get away with it.

Friday

Today I licked my bottom. It's a hobby and boy, do I need a hobby. (I gave up on the Create and Craft stuff. God, that was boring). I lick my bottom quite a lot, if I'm honest. I'm a very clean cat, although I don't just do it to be clean.

I am worried about Europe and I'm worried about us. What will happen if this Brexit nonsense goes ahead? I'll be okay; it doesn't really affect cats much, as far as I can tell, but a lot of people are going to be worse off. What happens if my family are in that position? I don't want there to be any reduction in my rations, although God knows, it wouldn't be a bad thing.

Saturday

There has been no post for 2 days.

Sunday

I want an Apple watch. The man has one on his scrawny wrist and the girl wants one for her birthday. You might say to yourself – why does a cat need an Apple watch? Well, why does anyone, you answer me that?

Monday

I am bored with my diet.

They have bought me a fake mouse. Do they think I am stupid? It looks a little bit like a mouse, except that it's round and has a little motor in it, and it's not real, obviously. It chunters along the floor and I'm supposed to chase it and play with it and pretend it's real. Give me strength. I shall have to go along with it, for a bit, I suppose, but if I see a real mouse loose about the house, I shall capture it and then they'll see the difference.

Tuesday

Every morning they do the vacuum cleaning. Usually her, occasionally him; the children - hardly ever.

Out of the cupboard it comes – Henry – that black and red machine with the coiled hose like a python. She plugs it in and drags the brush over the carpet. I have to run and hide and cover my ears with my paws to try and drown the sound. Sometimes, I fancy a lie-in, to sleep for 19 hours in each day, instead of my usual 18. But no, those minute flecks of dust must be hoovered up. It doesn't matter how early they have to get up or get out of the house, she has to have her vacuuming done – I swear to God that woman has OCD like you wouldn't believe.

Friday

I am going to the vet. They haven't told me, but I can guess. They have the basket ready. They've hidden it and think that I don't know but I do. I'm not stupid, you know, or blind. I'll play around for a bit, hide under the bed, jump on a wardrobe, go behind the sofa. I don't have to but it's sport for me and it annoys them. There's not much left for me so I might as well have some sport. 'Come here, darling,' they say, in that irritating, whiny, babyish way of theirs, as if that makes a difference.

Later

It was the vet: I was right, as I knew I would be. The vet had cold hands and stuck that thermometer up my arse. 'Arse' – not a nice word is it? But it will do, and you know what I mean. She just lifted up my tail, without so much as a by your leave, and shoved it in. Oh, the indignity. Mind you, it felt nice, for a bit. Then I had an injection. I don't know what it was; they didn't tell me, and I couldn't read the label on the bottle. The needle hurt a bit, but I'll get over it. 'This is just going to be a little prick,' said the vet. They always make that joke and I get so sick of it.

Saturday

I share my home with hangers-on, bugs, things that go dump in the night. Flies and bees and occasional wasps – which I hate, by the way, as you know. And chuggi-pigs and tiny, slivery, slithery things that leave a trail of slime near the back door as they desperately make a dash for it before I catch them, and even more when I've swallowed them. They taste a bit like oysters. Not that I've ever tried an oyster.

<u>Later</u>

This afternoon I watched 2001: A Space Odyssey[24]. Yes, I know it's an old film, but I was flicking through the channels and it came on. I don't know much about space, as you can imagine, having lived most of my life in a house in West Wickham, never seeing the world outside; have I told you that? Boy, do those first 20 minutes go on! The apes seemed quite life-like to me, although I've never seen a real one – I assume they were actors in suits, although they jumped around like apes and made grunting ape-noises which got a bit wearing after a while. And then one picks up a bone and they start fighting and one of the apes kills an animal with it – was it a tapir? I'm not sure, I suppose it could have been an actor in a tapir suit, but it was certainly good acting.

I sat, or to be more accurate, sort of slouched in that cat way, on the sofa while watching and had a good lick of my private parts while it played. Anyway, surely that bone would break, wouldn't it, because they're quite brittle, bones? I thought it was clever when it flew up in the air and turned into a space-ship. This is how humans imagined space and the universe back in 1968 – well, how Kubrick imagined it anyway. Cats see things differently and we have more experience. Humans think the universe is designed for them; I have news for you guys - it wasn't. And no, it wasn't designed for cats; I'm not that cat-centric. There is order in the universe; it follows immutable laws of physics and chemistry and biology and so forth, but within that it's random, things don't happen for a reason, they happen because they happen.

And the big, black monolith. Give me strength. That isn't the key to the universe. Read on and maybe you'll learn what it is, maybe I'll share it with you. And then again, maybe I won't.

However, there are scenes in the film that were breath-taking; it is filming of the highest order. And the way Kubrick marries his images with Strauss and the other bits of classical music was wonderful. But the ending doesn't work. The last 20 minutes, I thought I was going to have a fit – all those flashing images and the swirling colours – it's like someone bought a computer and discovered a graphics programme having dropped some acid (which is probably what did happen) and then spent hours gazing at the screen in wonder thinking they'd found God.

But the scene where Keir Dullea crawls into HAL's brain and starts removing bits of memory and HAL gradually loses awareness and consciousness and fades away and then starts singing 'Daisy, Daisy, give me your answer do...'[25] Is that what death is like, I wonder? Your memory fades away and then you start singing about bicycles and then it all fades to black? I could live with that type of dying.

So; boring, fab, decent, fab, fab, boring, fab, rubbish. That's my review.

My private parts tasted good though. And then I had some fish.

Sunday

What are friends? What are mates? I read about them, I see programmes about them, but I've never had one. Pitiful, isn't it? No best friend forever, no best mate, no group of like-minded cats to share jokes and memes and post stupid stories to on Facebook.

Later

I'm going to try and escape. I watched a film this afternoon – The Great Escape[26], maybe you've heard of it – about a group of British prisoners-of-war who escape from a German camp by digging a tunnel. It doesn't end well but mine will.

I'm starting in the cupboard under the stairs, where they keep their coats and shoes and a lot of other mess. There's some damp in there and the paint has flaked away, and the plaster is crumbling. They won't fix it, they never fix anything, the slobs. But at least it means that my gradual escape plan can come to fruition without fear (unlike those brave POWs and Steve McQueen), of being discovered.

The family went out this afternoon; Sunday lunch in some not too expensive pub and then a walk through a forest that I'll never see, I shouldn't wonder. So, I thought I'd make a start.

God.

It was hot in there and hard work – harder than I thought it would be. Unlike the POWs I couldn't strip down, my fur is not removable, in case you didn't know. I pawed at the crumbling plaster and made a small hole. It was about 2 inches wide and a half-inch deep and took me 2 hours, until exhaustion and lack of willpower forced me to stop.

In the film, they cover the hole with a wooden horse. I couldn't find a horse, but this family has a collection of stuffed animals, so I found an old, brown bison that no-one plays with and used that. I wonder if they'll notice. As far as I can tell, these animals are not, and were not, real. But I'm not certain of that. I do have a slight worry that when I die, they'll have me emptied like an Egyptian Mummy and then stuffed with cotton wool and left to rot on their bed with the cow and the monkey, the penguin and the bison, the Harry Potter beasts and the collection of brown and black bears.

Maybe life here isn't so bad.

Or I could knot some sheets together and lower myself from the bathroom window. Who am I kidding? Like Steve McQueen[27], I'll never get away. But never let me stop dreaming of my great escape. If you stop dreaming, you stop living.

<u>Monday</u>

I haven't always lived here, you know. I've always been a prisoner, but this hasn't always been my prison. I was at a cat charity before this and before that I lived with an old lady. I can't remember where I was before her.

She was nice, the old lady, but she got ill. I think that's when I learned to read and write. She didn't mean to neglect me, but her mind started to go, and her memory. And then she didn't know who I was or what I was. And she didn't feed me. I'd meow and scratch at the cupboards and scratch her sometimes, but I don't think she understood what I was doing or why and I couldn't talk. Of course, I can't talk now but that's different; I don't need to. I found out what was wrong with her. I looked it up on the computer, typed in her symptoms and then looked it up on Wikipedia. She had dementia, so it wasn't her fault, she didn't deliberately stop feeding me or neglect me, it just got to the point where she no longer knew what do or how to do it or when. Sometimes she'd feed me and then 10 minutes later she'd feed me again and then again and again. And I was greedy and fat, so I ate the food she left. But then she wouldn't feed me at all and it didn't matter how much noise I made or jumped on her lap or licked her face or slunk around her legs rubbing against her feet, she still didn't feed me. And then I'd get hungry and weak and my tummy would hurt.

And then she died. I was sad; she was nice to me and it wasn't her fault she got sick.

So, that's how I ended up at the cat charity. They kept me inside too. They said I was an indoor cat. But I wasn't an indoor cat; the old lady had kept me in, but I didn't ask for it, it wasn't my choice. She did that. She lived on a main road and she worried I would run out in the traffic and get killed. Why would I do that? I'm not stupid and I know what cars look like. And you need a bit of risk in your life, don't you?

Tuesday

I've been exploring. You'd think, after having lived here most of my life, that there would not be an inch of this house that I have not explored, discovered, crept into, sidled along, sniffed out, observed, scratched at or pawed at; but you'd be wrong. Today I discovered a secret passageway. Secret to me, but I rather suspect that the owners don't know of it either. This is a large house, old and strange. I was in the dining room where I spend much of my time. It's warm with a nice carpet (a bit frayed) and an open fire. I lie on the carpet in front of the fire and sleep the sleep of the just while the family shuffle around or tickle my tummy and run their fingers through my fine fur. Sometimes sparks shoot out of the fireplace and it's a bit scary, but it's a risk I'll take.

But today the house was empty, apart from me. There is wooden panelling on either side of the fireplace, old but nicely made and in good condition. Occasionally I'll rub up against the panelling and scratch an itch and I was doing that earlier. I must have leaned against something because a section of the panelling slid silently open on some hidden hinges, revealing a passageway. It was maybe a foot square so big enough for me (just – I'm quite fat, as you know) with enough room for an animal to crawl into. I entered. It was gloomy but not dark and some light must enter from somewhere because it stretched ahead for some distance and a faint glow illuminated the walls. I went slowly. I felt scared and nervy, I'm not sure why – the fear of the unknown I suppose. I pushed further in. I half suspected the panel to swing back behind me, interring me in some tomb, like you see in the films or that Sherlock Homes story, the Musgrave Ritual[28], but that didn't happen. It was cold in there – people think cats don't feel the cold because of our fur and stuff, but we do.

The passage continued. Who would have thought there would be space in the house, but it did. After a while I came to a small room. It was tiny, maybe 3 feet square with a low ceiling. I could stand up, obviously, but a dog would struggle. There was a blanket and a torch which didn't work and a small box which may have contained food. There were cracks in the walls which is how the light came in. It was like that Leonard Cohen song[29], one of my favourites – 'there is a crack in everything, it's how the light gets in'. Could Leonard Cohen have lived in this house? That seemed unlikely – to my knowledge he had never visited West Wickham and this space would have been too small for him.

I looked it up on Wikipedia. Apparently, during the time of Cromwell, many years ago, it was against the law to keep a cat as a pet. Some people (you'll call them brave, I call them traitors), defied the law. They were known as 'catolics' and they would build secret spaces, known as 'pussy holes' where their pets would hide. Troops of Cromwell's supporters would tour the country, searching for pussy holes and secret cat hordes and many catolics[30] were persecuted and put to death as a result. If you ask me, they deserved it.

I lay down and licked my fur. It seemed as good a place as any. I cleaned my paws and rubbed spittle on them and cleaned my ears and as much of my head as I could reach, as I pondered this mystery. And then I licked my private parts. When in doubt, lick your private parts – that's my philosophy and I recommend it.

I was a prisoner in my own house, but it seems I had not been the only one. What must their life have been like — here in this small room with nothing but walls and a floor for company, a small blanket to keep them warm, scraps of food? At least I had all the facilities of the house at my disposal — the wi-fi, television, DAB radio, computers, the many books, their meagre collection of vinyl, my warm carpet by the fire, the people who clearly loved me and looked after me. Maybe my life was not as bad as I have made out.

I left after a while, when my fur was clean and I had finished pondering this one of life's mysteries. I returned to the rug in front of the fire. The panel closed behind me and there was nothing to indicate that it had been there. Had I dreamt it?

Slop for dinner again.

I hate my life.

The children stopped reading the journal at this point and went looking for the passage and the tiny room. The panelling is still there in the dining room by the fireplace and they tapped at each of the panels, like detectives do, listening for hollow sounds or whatever detectives are listening for, but there was nothing different, no tell-

tale sounds or lack of them and no hidden door on hidden hinges. Maybe Sir Ian made it all up or maybe the previous owners found the passage-way and blocked it. Who knows? We looked up 'Catolics' on Wikipedia and there was nothing, which is suspicious.

<u>Wednesday</u>

Top 10 scratching locations:

1. Brand new dark grey Ikea sofa in the living room – I thinks it's called Tidafors. I call it Madeforclaws.
2. Fairly new pale blue Laura Ashley sofa in the dining room.
3. Stair carpet, third step from the bottom.
4. Green armchair.
5. Landing carpet outside the bathroom.
6. Stair carpet, fourth step from the bottom.
7. Pale grey foot-stool.
8. Brown armchair.
9. Off-cut of carpet which they put down beneath my toilet tray – but only if I need a scratch after I've had a dump.
10. Stair carpet, third step from the top.

<u>Thursday</u>

They were talking last night, around the dinner table, the boy playing with his phone, the girl playing with hers, me on the sofa pretending to sleep and listening to their conversation.

'I've seen this charity,' the woman says.

'Oh yeah?' the man says, watching You've Been Framed and not paying attention, like he never does.

'It supports cats overseas,' she continues. 'They call it cat fostering; you pay money every month and they send you photos and updates about your cat and your money pays for their upkeep.'

'Is that a joke?' he says.

'No, why should it be?'

'Well, what about our cats, British cats, home-grown cats, surely we should support them first before we worry about foreign cats?'

'British cats? Foreign cats? What are you on about? Cats are just cats; they don't have a nationality – cats in this country aren't British cats, they're just cats in Britain.

And cats in other countries are just cats in other countries, they're not foreign.'

'Anyway, we can't afford it.'

'It's only £15 a month. Cats are cheaper in the Third World.'

'Well, okay then. But pick a nice one, a pretty one. I don't want some miserable, hideous cat, ugly as sin, with attitude; we've got one of them already.'

£15 a month, diary! I could do with that money. Get some more stuff on Amazon. And I'm not hideous.

Sunday

Cats have nine lives, so it is said. I've just lost one; let me tell you how it happened.

I partially ate a dish-washer tablet.

That was a mistake. How was I to know? I started foaming at the mouth. I think they thought I had rabies and I played along with that, jumping away when I saw some water[31] – how I laughed (inwardly, of course), at that. They say a cat has nine lives. I've now got 8 left.

The tablet tasted disgusting, by the way. Not as bad as one of those cat treats, but not far off. I would not recommend it.

Wednesday

Places I will never see:

- Lake Annecy

- The canals of Bruges

- Mont Ventoux

- The Hermitage in St Petersburg

- Rolling, tumbling, scrub-strewn parched wild animal grazing grasses in Africa

- The flowing white, ice floed, chill dampness of the Arctic; polar bears and Arctic foxes, flabby seals and furred up Eskimos

- Junks in Hong Kong

- Charles Bridge in Prague in a cold, cold winter, -6 and the breath frozen in icy mist as it leaves your mouth, iced up whiskers and needing my claws to stop slipping on the frozen streets

45

- Venice and the streets full of water, over-priced gondolas zig-zagging along

- London, Paris, Geneva, Amsterdam, Warsaw – in fact, any European city

- The Lake District, Yorkshire, Malham Cove and Gordale Scar, Ribblehead Viaduct, Whitby and Robin Hood Bay, York Minster

- Auschwitz

- Apes on the Rock of Gibraltar

- Table Mountain

- The Marianas Trench – it's in the Pacific Ocean and is the deepest part of the ocean.

- Clouds scudding – scudding, I love that word.

- New-mown grass, wet leaves, freshly tilled earth, the delicate buds of spring flowers, drifting rain, the salty tang of the sea, fast-flowing, cold river water, branches heavy with snow, rising sap, pollen.

How do I know all this, you ask? What do I know of the world, whom only the inside of this house has seen? I'm not stupid, you know. I can work the remote, I watch the documentaries, I see David Attenborough from the vantage point of someone's warm lap, one eye closed and the other drinking it in and waiting to be fed.

I'll never walk the surface of the moon in a big cat space-suit, or dive beneath the waves of the Great Barrier Reef in my little cat wet-suit, or swing through the tropical trees of Costa Rica or walk to Macchu Picu, paddle my kayak across the Torres Straits, play pooh-sticks in the Ashdown Forest, go island hopping in the Caribbean, cruise the Baltic in a giant ship as their very own ship's cat, or drift down the Nile, lazily sipping top of the milk from my very own gold-plated saucer.

Let's face it, and I am facing it, I'll never see anything, do anything, go anywhere, be anyone, break a heart, mend a fence, father a child, bury a parent, save a child from drowning or eat a peach. (Well, I might try a peach).

Thursday

Boring. Nothing happened. I took in a parcel for next door. I don't think I'll tell them.

Boring. Nothing happened. I think the radiator in the living room needs bleeding.

Saturday

Who is the Patron Saint of cats?

I watched Some Like it Hot[32] – I love that movie. Tony Curtis, Jack Lemmon, Marilyn Monroe – have they ever been better? Billy Wilder persuades Marilyn – a clever girl who everyone regards as silly and innocent and naïve – to play a girl who's silly and innocent and naïve and she's so clever, and such a brilliant actress, that she does it – and you think she's acting! Genius! And George Raft, who was a friend of gangsters, plays a gangster. If you haven't seen it, you are in for a treat. It's in black and white, by the way.

Monday

The window cleaner came today. He's getting on a bit now and struggles on the ladder. Sometimes I like to hide behind a curtain and leap out at him, just as he's standing on the top step of the ladder and reaching over with his squeegee thing. He always gives a little jump, but I haven't made him fall off his ladder yet. I shall keep trying.

I know it's childish, but I can be childish, can't I?

Anyway, it's his own fault. I saw on the news that there are some new health and safety regulations and he's not supposed to be up a ladder.

Sunday

These people are so lazy that they can't be bothered to do their own gardening and so they employ a gardener. He comes once a fortnight and stays a couple of hours. I watch him sometimes, to make sure he doesn't get up to any tricks and actually does what he's paid to. He works quite hard, raking up leaves, mowing the lawn, carting the cuttings away, sweeping, some plant pruning and general tidying up.

Frankly, I don't see why the man who lives here doesn't do it, or the woman; they're hardly rushed off their feet, looking after me and the kids. Sheer laziness. Or the boy and the girl, they could do it.

Monday

Big excitement at breakfast. There was (almost) a fire in the kitchen. It happened like this:

The man is on a diet (he's not as fat as me but, put it like this, it wouldn't hurt him to lose a few pounds – I can be quite catty if I want to be), and has stopped stuffing his face with toast and butter every breakfast. Instead, he makes an omelette.

This morning, he heated the frying pan, put some rapeseed oil in and heated it up. I think he put too much oil in and then swirled the pan too much because some oil splashed out and ignited on the cooker surface. Whoosh! Big flames! Cue much shouting and cursing, major panic, faffing about, until he put the fire out.

These people!

Tuesday

There is sickness in the house. I'm not sure how serious it is. The man hasn't been to work – he lies in bed moaning and occasionally being sick. He also has diarrhoea and rushes to the toilet. Boy, it stinks; worse than mine, if that's possible.

She fusses around him, bringing him cups of tea and constantly asks him if he's all right. It gets a bit wearing.

He's not a lot of trouble but I could do without it.

I hope she doesn't get sick – who'll prepare my 6 (or 7) meals a day and change my tray when it's full? The kids never do it (if you ask me, there's a certain lack of discipline in their lives and they are both incredibly lazy – not my business maybe, but I do live here). The man doesn't do much either, if you ask me. He obviously thinks that because he goes to work, he doesn't have to do anything around the house – which strikes me as a rather sexist, old-fashioned attitude. He's not what you call a new man and if you ask me, it won't be long before he's an old man. And then what will he do?

Wednesday

The sickness continues.

The girl has taken to her bed now. Between ourselves, I don't think she's really ill but I daren't say anything – not that I can, of course. Well, I could but I won't.

Thursday

The man's gone to work. Thank the Lord – he was getting on my nerves, moaning and puking all the time and disappearing off to the toilet 10 times a day and shouting at the woman to bring him a cup of tea. Frankly, it's better if it's just me and the woman in the house – more peaceful and we get on fine together. And I get fed regularly.

Wednesday

They got rid of the plastic mat under my toilet tray. Not before time. Little puddles of wee used to collect on it where I missed the tray and then they slid off onto the carpet underneath, which had started to smell. Smell! It stank, and I don't know why they didn't do something about it before.

Anyway. They've bought a couple of off-cuts of carpet which they've put on the floor to cover up the stains. The smell is still there but now you can't see it. They seem to think that makes it better: it doesn't.

Thursday

Some Mormons[33] came to the door. The woman answered it and stood on the door-step, chatting to them for ages. Does she not realise that's fatal? They'll convert her next and then what? She'll move to Utah and be one of 6 wives, like Henry VIII, only a woman, if that makes sense.

I remember when she toyed with Scientology[34] and covered the house with pictures of Tom Cruise and John Travolta and then there was a short period when she thought of converting to Islam. She started wearing a burka and refused to eat pork. This was at the time of Ramadan and she was supposed to fast from dawn to dusk which was never going to work. And it didn't; it lasted one day and then she took off the burka and had a big cooked breakfast.

Another time, she discovered Buddhism and became a vegetarian and spent her time sitting cross-legged on the floor wittering about karma and then making some odd, chanting noise. Thankfully, that phase didn't last. And the other day she was talking about getting a tattoo.

She needs to have an affair.

The girl wants a tattoo. She keeps making these mad suggestions – phrases she reads in novels, bits of Shakespeare, flowers, lines from poems, something in

Arabic, or a lion. I blame social media but I'm warming to the idea. I quite like small, tasteful tattoos – not tramp stamps, obviously, or sleeves.

Cats don't have tattoos for a few reasons:

1. We're covered in fur, so you wouldn't see it.

2. Most cats (including me) don't like the sight of blood

3. We can never decide what to get

<u>Friday</u>

We have this postman who is always on the phone. You can hear him down the street, shouting at people on his stupid phone. People can be so inconsiderate. It's usually when I'm having my mid morning nap and it invariably wakes me up.

I was thinking of lying in wait and making a run for it when they open the door for another one of their Amazon parcels, but they always make sure the door to whichever room I'm lurking in is shut so I never get the chance.

And do I really want to escape?

I say I do and I think I do and it's what I feel I ought to do, and I should do and I would do if I got the chance, but do I really? Really?

Maybe not. Maybe I'm just pretending and fooling myself, trying to make my life seem more interesting and me braver than I really am.

Be careful what you wish for – ancient Chinese proverb. But it makes a lot of sense. Fulfilment is not always better than anticipation. What would happen to you if all your dreams came true and you got everything you ever wanted? Would you be like the fisherman's wife always wanting more, or the lottery winner who bought a private jet and crashed on their first flight – all their dreams and most of their money gone in a puff of smoke and skidding tyres?

And anyway, what would I do and where would I go in that big, wide world?

Maybe home is where your 6 (or 7) dinners are and where people love you or pretend to love you. I'd take pretend love over no love, every time.

Saturday

Existential interlude.

What came before the Big Bang?

In the beginning, there was nothing, just a ball of matter, incredibly dense and the Big Bang exploded that ball of matter and the universe was created as it spread outwards. And it is still spreading and will go on spreading. And before the Big Bang, you ask? Ahhhhhh. What I believe is that there was no 'before' – before is a concept that only exists if time exists and as there was no time, there was no before. Humans can't grasp this, but cats can. We sit around (if there is more than one of us, which in this house there isn't, as I'm the only cat, but still), and we lick our private parts and yawn and sharpen our claws on carpets and upholstery and we ponder the mysteries of the universe. And then we sip some milk, or fornicate (not me, obviously), and sleep the sleep of the just.

<u>Later</u>

They bought me some jewellery. They went shopping and returned with a new collar, but I call it cat jewellery. It's soft and black and there's a silver disc which hangs from it, which has my name on it. Not <u>my</u> name; the name they've given me. My true name is a secret which only another cat can know. And I don't know any other cats.

Sunday

The end of all things.

Sunday bloody Sunday. Depressed, down, in the dumps. They've gone and left me – again. I heard them talking, little whispers in quiet corners when they think I'm not listening, or maybe they think I can't understand. But I'll catch them out. They whisper to each other in cat whispers, but I can read their lips, the swine. Garden centre, tea shop, Sainsburys, all the detritus of their hum-drum lives but so far beyond what I can do, it might as well be the Azores or the Gobi Desert or St Helena.

I pissed on the carpet on the stairs. That'll teach 'em. I wish they'd get the message. They just think I'm incontinent or getting old or 'poor pussy' – they don't get that it's a protest, my little revolt, my deepening anger over how they treat me.

The fools! They've bought some strange smelling scented stuff – it sits on the window-sill above where I piss and there are little sticks stuck in the neck of the bottle like long tooth-picks and they suck up the smell of lavender or basil or turmeric or whatever the hell it is and release it into the atmosphere to counter-act the over-powering smell of my urine which now permeates every nook and cranny of my prison. It won't work. Piss, lavender, piss, lavender, piss, lavender, piss, piss. Piss wins, every time. My patience is greater than theirs and my bladder can re-fill and re-fill and re-fill more than their glass bottles ever will.

I know it's childish. But they started it.

Tuesday

I watched a documentary last night, while sitting on the girl's lap, about the world and pollution. A world made of plastic is what we'll end up with, if we're not careful. The amount of plastic they get through in this house is criminal and the kids never do any re-cycling, they just throw it in the bin. After they've all gone to bed I sort through their rubbish and put it into the correct re-cycling bins. Paper goes in the paper pile (hope it doesn't blow away, ha ha), plastic goes in the plastic pile, glass goes with glass. But the little square cat-food trays (i.e. that contain my dinner), what do you do with them? And the little dribbles of brown liquid swilling around the bottom after the tray has been emptied into my bowl; where does that go?

It's a mystery, wrapped in an enigma, hidden in a conundrum, bound by the unknown.

Wednesday

Vegetarians and vegans? I mean, why? Why would you bother?

I don't get it.

I have learned to open a tin of food. I shall keep this discovery to myself. Why should I do all the work?

Thursday

There has been a power cut. We were in darkness most of the day plus the television didn't work, the Wi-Fi was off, and the fridge stopped working, so my cream was warm and smelt funny. It was miserable.

Friday

Newspapers are no longer delivered. I know the print media is dying – I watched a programme about it on YouTube but still one wonders...are they short of money?

<u>Saturday</u>

I saw a ghost last night and it scared the living daylights out of me – to be honest, diary, I'm only just getting over it.

It happened like this:

It was a dark and stormy night – no, really it was. There was heavy rain (I've never felt rain) and it lashed against the windows and the roof, and there was a heavy wind (I've never felt wind, outside) which blew in powerful gusts and I was worried that the big oak tree in the garden would blow over, and there was thunder and lightning, in fact everything; like I said, stormy.

They'd all gone out to Pizza Express – the woman had a 2 for 1 voucher – she loves her vouchers and the girl loves the cannelloni while the man always has a great big American Hot pizza with extra pepperoni, the pig. (I know because they talk about it endlessly when they come in).

Anyway, it was late and dark, and I was upstairs, asleep on the girl's pillow – my 3rd favourite place to sleep, if you remember diary. The room was dark, and the curtains were closed but not completely, so a bit of light from the street lamp seeped in, like a stain. I was lying there, my paws tucked under me in that cute way they always like, my right cheek resting on one paw, and I was dreaming of filthy girl cats, as I often do. Something woke me, and I opened one eye, as cats do. I could hear creaking, like a wooden shutter slowly swinging back and forth on rusty hinges. From where I lay, at the back of the room, under the radiator, its soft warmth enveloping my back, I had a clear view of her bedroom door, which was open.

As I lay there, one eye open, drowsy, the dregs of my dirty dream still dancing through my mind, I saw a pale figure move swiftly across the hallway past the open door. It had four legs and slunk in a slinking kind of way, with whiskers and a cat's features. You could have knocked me down with a feather, if I'd been standing up. As it passed the door, it turned its head and looked at me, with a little ghostly smile on its chops and I swear it winked.

I leaped up and arched my back as I straightened up and yawned – no need to rush, I thought.

I sort of sidled to the door, trying to look nonchalant and just as I got to the door I leaped through, like a scalded cat (which I wasn't but am, if you know what I mean).

Nothing.

The landing was bare, no cat but me.

What does it mean, diary? Am I not alone in this house after all? Do I share my prison with another? Or were there others before me, and this was the ghost of one of them?

It's a mystery.

<u>Sunday</u>

When will they buy a new sofa? This one is scratched to bits. They take no pride in their stuff. It think it's him; he just doesn't notice stuff – I swear he's in a world of his own half the time. All he thinks about is his bloody bikes. What does he see in them?

He re-arranged the furniture in the living room yesterday. God, did that create some arguments.

'What have you done?' she said.

'I switched the sofas around,' he said. 'What do you think?'

'Alright,' she said, in a tight-lipped kind of way.

'Don't you like it?' he said.

'Why do you say that?'

'You don't seem very enthusiastic.'

'Why didn't you ask me?'

'Ask you what?'

'About moving the furniture around, instead of just going ahead and doing it? I would have asked you. I would have discussed it with you. But you just go ahead and do it.'

'Well, do you like it?'

'That's not the point. You should have spoken to me first.'

'I can move it back.'

'That's not what I'm saying.'

'So, do you like it then?'

'It's alright.'

And so it goes on.

Monday

It is getting lighter in the mornings. When will the clocks go forward? I am confused by time, as by so many things. Where does that hour come from and where does it go? And what will happen when we leave Europe? Will they still be an hour ahead of us, or can we take that hour back, along with sovereignty, control, blue passports, security of our borders, freedom from interference by the European Court and those unelected, bureaucratic busybodies in Brussels?

Tuesday

I will never understand geometry. Squares and rectangles, I get, and a circle is obvious. But what's a trapezoid? What's a cone? What's the difference between an isosceles triangle and a triangle? What's a plane? Who was Euclid?[35] And Pythagoras?[36] What is pi? And tangents and cosines? Anyone have any idea?

The weather never changes in here.

Wednesday

I saw the space station pass. At least, I think it was the space station. It was night, they'd all gone to bed. I sat, as I often do, on the window seat in the conservatory. There's a soft cushion there, now drenched in my cat smell, fluffy with my moulted hairs, it's a favourite spot.

I can look up, through a gap in the curtains, to the glowing pin-pricks of light in the night sky. Occasionally I see a plane, winking lights winking in the gloom, track its steady path to Heathrow or heading out to the Continent, destination who knows where. I do my best to pick out the stars and the few constellations that are visible through my small patch of glass. I don't understand constellations. You look at a picture in a book and it says this pattern is the 'Great Bear' or 'Orion's Belt' or whatever it is, and I think, I can't see that, I can't see a belt, I can't see a bear, great or otherwise. I'm just seeing stars.

Anyway.

I saw a faint light, moving across the sky. I bet it was the space station and it got me thinking: what do they do up there, as the long days morph into long nights, and they're trapped, round and round, round and round, for days, weeks, months, years sometimes, if you're Russian? Their lives must be a lot like mine; eat, sleep, shit, more sleep, eat, another shit – if it's a good day. And then they come home and nobody cares any more – they've seen it all before and now they're just another astronaut who spent six months on the space station playing computer games.

Thursday

I hate Thursdays. I was reading G K Chesterton's The Man Who Was Thursday[37] the other day and it got me thinking: which is the worst day? Everyone moans about Sunday but Sunday's okay. Thursday is my problem day. It's not the beginning of the week – that's Monday (or Sunday in some cultures) or the end of the week – that's Friday or Sunday if you prefer, and Wednesday is the middle of the week. Saturday's always fun so that leaves Tuesday and Thursday and Thursday's mine. Ergo, or whatever the Latin is.

Friday

He bought a shed. He calls it a 'garden room' and she calls it her 'retreat', but really, it's a glorified shed. I watched the workmen erecting it – trapped behind my glass, like the specimen I am.

It looks nice, painted green (although I hate that colour), with electrics and heating and a TV, an armchair, a desk where he'll sit and pretend to write his boring cycling stories and she'll pretend to write her angst-ridden short stories, with her deathless prose which no-one will ever read. God, I sound bitter.

Don't be bitter, peeps. It's not very attractive.

I wish I had a shed, my own private space – a home of my own, with a private toilet – my own secret pussy hole, that I could disappear into.

Who am I kidding?

No shed for Sir Ian, not in this life, anyway.

Saturday

I see no benefit in digital radio.

I received a letter; cat post is like human post - not great but it works, eventually.

It turned out to be a chain letter. Why am I being sent a chain letter, who am I going to send it on to?

'Send to 10 of your friends,' it said. Why do they mock me like that? They know I don't have 10 friends – I don't even know 10 cats, never mind 10 cat friends.

And what will happen to me if I don't send it on?

'You'll have no friends,' it says. That scares me no end.

Later

The Great Gatsby is not as good as everyone thinks. I read it in an afternoon while they went ice-skating.

Fitzgerald is a fine stylist, but I sometimes wonder if his story doesn't sink under the weight of his style. I prefer his short stories. The Cat as Big as the Ritz[38] – about a giant cat that morphs into a Parisian hotel, is my favourite (joke).

Sunday

Under-floor heating does not count as progress. The Romans had under-floor heating. And flushing toilets. And central heating. And built many of the roads that people travel on still. I watched a programme about them.

And the Chinese invented paper.

Tuesday

I'm going to try and send a message in a bottle. I have a bottle – it belonged to the girl and used to contain Evian water. And I have a message:

'Dear Sir or Madame (it helps to be polite)

I am a cat imprisoned in a house in West Wickham in Kent. Please send help. No reasonable offers declined.

Yours etc

Sir Ian (the cat)'

I shall put the message in the bottle but how to throw it in the sea? I am nowhere near the sea.

I know. I shall leave it with the other rubbish and they can put it out with the recycling and then when it is recycled, someone will read a message and come and rescue me. Sorted!

The children found the bottle in the garden, hidden in some bushes. The message was still in it. We have taken the message out and framed it; it is on the wall in our hallway.

<u>Thursday</u>

Water is over-rated. It's all I'm ever given.

Why don't they try me on something different? I heard someone on the telly talking about a 'medium, flat-white, skinny mocha with soy milk'. I have no idea what it is (and I'm not sure they did), but I fancy trying one.

Or a coffee, a coke, gin, orange juice, apple juice, pineapple juice, tomato juice, any bloody juice frankly, a nice sloe gin, cider, rum, a milkshake, J2o, hot chocolate, green tea, peppermint tea, camomile tea, any bloody tea or even an occasional beer would be nice.

But no, I'm the cat, so I get water and occasionally a little cream. I'm the cat who occasionally gets the cream – would you trade places with me?

Of course, you wouldn't.

Friday

I played with a bit of string. However, despite what you may think, cats do not enjoy playing with string. But what choice do I have? These people don't seem to own a chess set, I'd rather stick needles in my eyes than play Monopoly; Cluedo is dull, the PlayStation is out of order and I can't work the table football. So, string it is. That's my string theory. (Joke).

I wonder what they keep in their safe? Maybe I should put my journal in there. At least it would be safe.

This is how my day breaks down:

- Sleeping

- Running around

- Eating – a lot

- Toilet

- iPad

- Journal

- Repeat

- Repeat

Later

The wi-fi is not working. It's annoying, there's a film I was hoping to catch on iPlayer, perhaps you know it – The Cat and the Canary[39]. Bob Hope plays the cat (joke).

I think we have mice. I expect you think I'd be pleased about that, but you'd be wrong. I hate mice; as far as I know, all cats hate mice. They're small and squishy with truncated arms and tiny legs and little red eyes like pin-pricks and they have little teeth which are too big for their little mouths and stick out the front. They think they're so clever, standing on their hind legs with their stuck-up noses, sniffing the air and twitching. And they eat crumbs. Crumbs! Have they no pride, no self-respect? Is it any wonder we chase them? And when we catch them it's so easy to kill them, they die so easily and with so little fight; that's why we leave their little torn and bloody bodies on the kitchen floor, so you can see how smart we are.

I have finished 50 Shades of Grey. It was terrible. I'd say it's pornography but it's worse than that. That is time I will not get back. I feel like hitting something. Or abusing something. Get me a mouse!

Chery Cole[40] will always be Cheryl Cole to me, no matter how many times she gets into another failed marriage. That's a bit catty, sorry.

Saturday

And so, the seasons change. How do I know? The grass is parched and no rain falls. The sky is a deep blue. The central heating is switched off, not to return now until the nights draw in. They eat salad for dinner and the fridge is full of water and the freezer full of ice cream. Do I get cold food? Does salad grace my plate? Am I offered a cooling drink with ice cubes floating? No, I do not, it does not, and I am not.

'Have you got sun-block on?' the woman says to him as he sets out on his bicycle.

'Carry some water,' the kids are told.

'We've run out of ice cream,' the kids say, with monotonous regularity.

And they go on holiday and I go to the cattery.

They are going to the sea-side: Swanage, in Dorset, they go every year. They rent a house for a week.

I wish I could go; I'd be no trouble. They could keep me inside, but I'd be beside the sea, I'd watch the sun set over the dancing cliffs, and dream of chasing sea-gulls and bringing one of those ugly, filthy, scavenging, scruffy birds to an early, watery grave. I could dream of a holiday romance with a dainty, delicate, ginger with soft paws, or a swarthy, smoky moggie with come-to-bed eyes, my come-to-bed pussy. I could bask on the balcony with the warm sun chasing patterns on my fur, while they drift in the cold, cold water and build sand-castles, or go for long walks over the hills to Dancing Ledge and Swire Head.

Forget it. Why do I still dream?

I'm off to the cattery.

I don't want to go, but they chase me down and shove me in that grubby cat basket and the locks close around me like the seal on my Pharaoh's tomb. I ride on the back seat of the car, too low to see anything out of the window and in any case, I'm facing the seat so all I catch a glimpse of is the dirty velour of the back seat of their ageing Vauxhall. It's not a long journey but I know not where, there are no land-marks to give me a clue, I am like John Paul Getty III, catnapped in Italy, about to lose my ear to impatient gangsters[41].

I am nervous, I can't help it. I wet myself.

The car rolls to a stop and someone lifts the basket. The basket is set down, I hear voices, the door is unlocked, and I am released into a new prison. A cold, cement floor, wire mesh, a little hut like a hermit in the woods, a grubby blanket, a shit tray (not even my own), a metal bowl of milk. Home for the next week. I bet the wi-fi doesn't work.

Sunday

Nothing happened. I ate, I slept, I shat, I stared through the wire.

Monday

Nothing happened. I ate, I slept, I shat, I stared through the wire.

Tuesday

Nothing happened. I ate, I slept, I shat (twice), I hear her singing through the wire[42].

Wednesday

Something happened.

She made contact. It happened like this:

I was doing my usual – pacing the cement floor of my little cell, dreaming of the world outside, when I heard a faint tapping sound. I turned around, sniffed the air, pricked my ears, nothing. I headed to the back of the cell and leaned against the bare, grey cinder-block walls. There it was again; an insistent tapping, like the sound of life's big clock ticking the seconds away. I listened closer. There was an insistent rhythm to the tapping and gradually I made out the words.

'Hello,' it started. 'Who's there.'

'Me,' I tapped.

'Who are you?'

'They call me Sir Ian.'

'Sir Ian?'

'Yes.'

'Strange name. Why?'

'I don't know.'

'Are you alone?'

'I'm always alone', I felt like replying but didn't. Instead, I said:

'Yes. What's your name?'

'They call me Tiddles.'

'I'm sorry,' I said.

'Why?'

'That's a terrible name.'

'Thanks.'

'Sorry.'

The tapping stopped. I had a shit and a nap.

Thursday

I had just finished my breakfast when I heard the tapping again.

'How long have you been here?' she asked.

'Four days. No, five, no, this is my sixth.'

'You don't seem very sure.'

'Sorry. You lose track of time in here. How about you?'

'I don't know, I've lost track of time. 6 months maybe, maybe more.'

'Why so long?'

'I live here. I suppose you're on holiday?'

'I wouldn't call it a holiday.'

'You'll be going home though, won't you? For some of us, this is our home.'

'You're right. Sorry.'

Friday

There was no tapping. I tapped but got no response. I slept and ate. No shit today.

Saturday

They came for me and took me home. They were hot and tired, tanned and grumpy. When we got home, they gave me some cat treats. As you know, I don't like them, but I ate them anyway; doesn't pay to be ungrateful.

I had a dream about Tiddles. I woke up feeling guilty and feeling myself.

Sunday

I miss the cattery. And Tiddles. She seemed nice. But - holiday romances – they never last, do they? Mine didn't.

Tuesday

A new cat has appeared in the garden.

I think I'm in love. She is unattainable (literally). Is she outside looking in or am I inside looking out? Or are we both outside looking in? Maybe love is always inside, and we are always outside, or vice versa. Who can say?

All I know is that I ache for her. She puts her paw against the glass from her side and I put my paw against the glass from my side and we are so close and yet so far away, we rub our noses, or we try to, but the glass mocks us and instead of her warm softness all I feel is the cold hardness of the glass.

I tell her she must wait for me and one day I will come to her, but she is wiser and more worldly in these matters than I and she knows that I mean well but don't speak the truth. I know that she will find another, and they will roll and tumble in the grass and each tumble will mean another part of my heart will shrivel and die. They think I am happy inside but bit by bit I am dying inside.

Love, love, love, love, love, love, love, love, love, love, love, love, love for another is all of life, it is life, it's why we're here and why we go on, even cats, it's not Whiskas and licking your private parts and a warm place by the fire and sleeping all day (although that's a small part of it) – we do that because we have no love in our lives.

Yes, the man and the woman, the boy and the girl, they love me or think they do, but I can't love them, not in the same way. I need my species and they won't give me that. They call it love but I call it hate.

Wednesday

I saw her again, in the garden. She saw me looking and turned away and killed a bird and ate it before my eyes.

79

I took a phone call from someone who was offering a cast-iron investment. Cast iron is so last year; I shall invest in gold. Kruggerands possibly (can you still get them?) or an ingot. Ingots sound nice.

Thursday

She wasn't there today.

I've been reading Watchtower[43] magazine. I'm not convinced. If I was looking at the afterlife I think Betterware[44] looks more fun.

Friday

She's gone and she's not coming back. I know it, I sense it, I feel it, I think it. I dared to dream for one small moment in time and then it's gone. Those that dream at night are one thing; dreamers in the day are to be feared, they may take their dreams and cast them into reality and scare us all[45]. I'm a night dreamer, not from choice but from necessity.

Dominos are (or is it Domino's is? I'm never sure) offering 2 for 1 on any large pizza. Pizza Hut are offering buy 1, get 1 free. I can't work out which is the better deal. I don't like pizza so it's academic, but it passed the time.

Saturday

I have started to do my banking online. It's more convenient and obviously, I was never able to get to the bank.

Sunday

I think someone has been reading my journal. I found some smudges on a few of the pages which weren't there before and I noticed the girl giving me funny looks when I went into the cupboard where my failed tunnel was. I caught her following me; I think she's trying to find out where I keep the journal and my pencils.

Monday

There is no God. There, I've said it. May God strike me down if I'm wrong. I always suspected I didn't have a soul and now I'm sure of it.

Tuesday

The colour green offends me. It's boring. It has no soul, like me. I prefer reds and golds, yellows, sometimes blues, occasionally orange and a bit of black around the edges. Not green though.

Wednesday

I can't finish Proust. And I can't start Finnegan's Wake. And I'm half-way through Gravity's Rainbow. I didn't get Catch 22, Lolita is pornography, Dickens is dull, Steinbeck is depressing, Julian Barnes is insufferably middle-class, Ian McEwan is over-rated, Tolstoy is too long, and so it goes on. Great literature is not always great literature. Ah, but Dostoyevsky, good old Fyodor, he never lets you down.[46]

Thursday

I don't see the point of dogs. What do they contribute to the sum of feline happiness? Nothing.

I watched a programme about the ancient Egyptians. It seems they worshipped cats. I totally get that. A bit of cat worship would suit me just fine. I mean, they like me, these people, the ones who think they own me – but they don't worship me. There are no sacrifices on the altar of my fur, no burnt offerings left by my shit tray, they don't say prayers to me, or sing hymns on a Sunday and wait for my blessing. But they should.

Imagine what I could do for them, what gifts could be theirs?

Friday

I think my iPod is broken; it won't shuffle. First world problems.

I have set up a Just Giving page. If you are a taxpayer, please tick the gift aid option. I shall use the money for a good cause.

Thursday

I have a problem with numbers. I don't like the number 6. I have decided to remove it and ignore it if I come across it. Please don't send me anything with the number 6 in it. I'll eat 5 daddy long-legs' legs, but I'll leave the sixth. I'll be like God, resting on the seventh day, only mine will be on the sixth. Imagine if God had decided to rest on the third or fourth day, instead of the seventh? How would our lives be different? Not mine, maybe, but yours, perhaps.

Friday

I think my hair is falling out. Did you ever see a bald cat? Me neither, but then I've seen few cats. I found clumps of hair on the sofa and stuck to the carpet. Is it mine, or is it the man's?

I wonder if the microwave waves are affecting me? I need some tests. Maybe the microwaves taught me to read and write and showed me how to dream and then made my hair fall out. It's a theory.

Saturday

How will I know if I'm agoraphobic? Maybe I am agoraphobic and couldn't go outside even if I was able to? What if the door was left open one day and I made a dash for it and froze at the open doorway, the fresh air so clean and clear I could taste it, and the bright sunshine warm on my dancing fur and the light breeze caressing the grass and the other cats lying in the bushes in wait, with presents and a massive welcome party, and I couldn't do it, I couldn't go out and ended up stalled and someone would find me, crouched in the open doorway and they would look at me and not say anything and slowly pull the door close. It would be like that scene in Godfather part II[47] where Al Pacino closes the door in Diane Keaton's face and she stands there, disappearing from view as her children disappear forever.

Or that final scene in The Third Man[48] – do you know the one?

Joseph Cotten leans on the jeep and waits by the road after Orson Welles has been buried and Alida Valli, she walks towards him, in long shot, down the dusty road, with graves on either side, her head held high, looking straight ahead and Cotten aches for her and thinks this is his chance, with Welles gone she can love him, but she keeps on walking and doesn't look at him and he watches as she swishes past and disappears into the distance and out of his life forever.

That's me – Joseph Cotten. Always on the edge of life. And that cat in the garden, whose name I don't know and will never know – she's Alida Valli.

<u>Sunday</u>

I am not in love any more. My love has gone away and left me all alone. I have been sitting here listening to country love songs and weeping. Will I ever find true love in these four walls? Hank Williams, Emmylou Harris, but my absolute favourite is Lucinda Williams' song 'Three days.'[49]

'Did you only love me for those three days?

And I have been so fuckin' alone

Since those three days.'

Monday

Today I was mostly sleeping. Cat napping.

I won £25 on the premium bonds. Why do I never win the big one? Why do I have some luck but not the luck I really need and want? It's a mystery.

I think television rots the mind. It certainly rotted mine. I tried to eat the TV remote control. That did not go down well.

I have learned that the word 'pussy' is a slang term for a lady's private parts. I can't decide whether I'm pleased about this but a little bit offended or offended but a little bit pleased. I will give it some more thought.

My eyesight is failing; I think I need glasses. Where can one get an eye test around here?

Thursday

There is nowhere left to scratch. You've seen my top ten: I've scratched the carpets and the stairs, the armchairs and the sofas, I tried the curtains, but I slipped down. It annoys them but what do they expect? Claws need sharpening in case I'm ever attacked by a vicious animal, although that isn't likely to happen in here, and

I have nowhere else to go. I'm genetically programmed to sharpen my claws. It's what we do.

I have run out of places to scratch. I have run out of worlds to conquer. I read somewhere that Alexander the Great[50] wept when he was told that there were no worlds left to conquer. No worlds left *that they knew about*, would be more accurate perhaps.

They bought me a scratching post. I won't use it. That will annoy them no end. I won't use it, *because it's a scratching post.* Do you think in the wild, a cat uses a scratching post? Of course they don't, they use the whole of their world. And I shall do the same.

Wednesday

Cat Ballou[51] is not a film about cats. Cat on a Hot Tin Roof[52] is also not about cats: Elizabeth Taylor was good though. Kathmandu is the capital of Nepal; nothing to do with cats. A 'cat 'o nine tails' was a whip used to flog sailors in the British Navy until the late 19th century. They didn't use a real cat. They used to use cat-gut to string tennis rackets. Was that real cat-guts or was it an expression? I never knew, and I still don't know. But I don't like to think of my ancestors' guts being used to string a tennis racket. I mean, what did they use to make the tennis balls?

Later

Another of my favourite expressions is 'no room to swing a cat.' I don't think there's a cat swinging room in this house; if there is I've not been in it. I've never really been a swinging cat if I'm honest. I'm very dull and ordinary. Although I can read and write.

There was a very interesting programme on the television last night. Unfortunately, I can't remember anything about it. It was about memory.

I've never been a fan of modern art. I just don't get it. I also think Van Gogh is over-rated.

There's been a small earthquake in the Philippines. I don't know where that is. I hope it's not nearby.

Why do humans walk upright while us lesser (better?) animals are on four legs?

I have started to appreciate the true sound of a vinyl record again. It really cannot be beaten. They have a meagre collection, but their choices are good ones.

A few Dylan, Joni Mitchell's Blue, Van Morrison's Astral Weeks and No Guru, No Method, No Teacher, Santana, a band called Pavlov's Dog[53] who I've never heard of and have no desire to find out, some Grateful Dead, Mumford and Sons – their well-known one[54], but I like it, The Who's Tommy and Quadrophenia, Counting Crows (love it), Leonard Cohen, The Doors' Riders on the Storm.

I have been listening to Cat Stevens. He doesn't sound like any other cat I've ever heard. 'Morning has Broken' is a bit twee for my liking. 'Fathers and Sons' – at least he has a father. (I too have a father, I just don't know who it is, or was).

I have decided not to celebrate Christmas this year. It is just getting too commercialised. Instead I will order myself a present from Amazon and eat a big meal – or eight.

Thursday

I am going to withdraw from the 4th dimension.

They are putting the clocks forward, but I shall not change mine. I refuse to be imprisoned by time as I am imprisoned by everything else.

And so, the seasons come and go in an unending cycle. But it will end, one day it will all end.

Wednesday

My teeth are not good. I have an abscess in one of my fangs and it hurts like a bastard. I wish they'd hurry up and make an appointment with the dentist. I may need dentures. It's all vanity I know, but I don't want dentures.

There is little to be said for dry food.

Thursday

I refuse to play the National Lottery. I regard it as a tax on the poor and the gullible.

I have never had a hair cut. Why is that? They have hair-cuts – their hair gets long, and they leave the house and come back and their hair is short.

So why don't cats need hair-cuts? I know our hair falls out when it's hot and we're moulting, or we have cancer. I mean, it must grow because it gets longer, so how does it get shorter? Another of life's great mysteries.

Friday

I am learning French. I don't know why as I have no-one to talk to but maybe that will change. I dream of French pussy, as I'm sure others do. Cat in French is chat. Maybe I can chat with a French cat. Or get a pen-friend – some filthy French moggie in stockings and come-to-bed eyes. I need to lie down.

Saturday

I have never taken a holiday.

I am withdrawing from Twitter. I am fed up with the abuse and the constant drivel. I am toning down my social media profile. But you can still follow my Instagram feed on #indoorcatworship.

Sunday

Global warming has not affected me so far. But I am concerned for the future of the planet. What if there are no houses left for cats to live in? That would be good. Or would it? Burning fossil fuels, methane gas, cutting down the Amazon rain-forest (Amazon does rain-forests?), filling the oceans with plastic, destroying the environment. Just because I'm a cat who never leaves the house, doesn't mean I don't think about these things. You're not the only ones who care.

Single-use plastic straws – they're an abomination.

What's a straw?

Monday

I wonder if I have dementia? I certainly have short-term memory loss and I often get confused. But how will I know?

I can remember the name of the Prime Minister (unfortunately) and I know what day it is and what I had for breakfast, but other things fade in and out of my memory, like a radio signal when the weather is bad, and the strong winds blow.

But does it matter? Lose your mind and you might lose your dreams.

Tuesday

I have a song in my heart, but I can't remember the words. I get so lonely sometimes that it hurts.

Later

Laps aren't comfortable.

Wednesday

I have fleas. Where do they come from? They are little, they say little and they smell. What purpose do they serve? I would flee but I have nowhere to go.

Thursday

I have created a race circuit on the ground floor. My PB (personal best) so far is 11 seconds. It is not the same as competing against someone else, but it will have to do.

Friday

Fur balls are not funny. I've heard all the jokes so don't bother. We get fur balls because we lick our fur and then we swallow it and hair can't be digested. Did you know that? You'll never find any hair in my shit. I should know; I looked. So, all the hair binds together in your stomach, into a ball, and after a while it gets too big and you have to puke it up and that's the fur ball. Not nice, I know, but such is a cat's life.

Saturday

I think my memory is going but I don't know where it's gone. I remember less now than I used to. And I can't remember what I've forgotten.

Did I write that already? I can't remember.

Sunday

I've never seen Star Wars and have no desire to, either.

Monday

TS Elliot[55] hated cats. I hate TS Elliot. However, I've always secretly enjoyed Sylvia Plath – you can never have enough angst in your life.

Tuesday

I hate labels. However, I am a mongrel cat. Nothing fancy about me. I hate Persians, Birmans, Siamese, and that other posh breed whose name I can never remember[56].

Wednesday

A catastrophe is a disaster, a traumatic event. I don't see why it should be named after a cat. Cats are not responsible for the world's ills.

Thursday

I've never seen Star Trek.

Friday

Stephen Fry doesn't do it for me. I could never watch QI; even with that Danish woman[57] now doing it.

Saturday

I have started talking to myself. This is not a good sign. I have nothing interesting to say. I was talking to myself yesterday and got bored with the conversation and sidled away. The other me didn't realise and carried on talking. Maybe I'm going mad.

Thursday

This place needs decorating. I don't know why I should live in squalor. The paint is faded and chipped, the kitchen is old and tired and the cupboard doors don't fit properly, the taps drip, the carpet is scuffed and streaked and stained with wee (mainly mine), doors are warped, curtain hooks are missing, there is dust everywhere, doors don't close cleanly, there are spider-webs in all the corners; what is wrong with these people?

Why does nobody in this house never put anything away? The place is a mess and no-one except me seems to care. Yesterday I nearly fell down the stairs when I tripped on one of their toys. I would have sued.

Always Thursday

Time has no meaning. The days have no meaning. Life has no meaning. Meaning has no meaning. It's later than you think.

Friday

Spotify is better than Apple Music.

Saturday

Foxes, diary, I ask you - foxes. I know I've never met one (I've never been outside in case you've forgotten), but I see them all the time, outside (or is it inside, we've had that debate). They seem brazen to me. Slinking around, with their long snouts, little eyes and bushy tails – and they're always ginger! I hate gingers. And they scavenge, too. And make a mess, in my garden. I mostly see them at night, when they think they're invisible – but not to me, as I can see in the dark, and occasionally sneak a carrot, if I see one lying around in the kitchen, so I can see even better, not that it helps, but still. And they slink around, through the bushes, the undergrowth, hiding behind the oak tree trunk, scrabbling at the compost bin and the food bin, dirty creatures. And at night, when I'm sleeping, I hear this unearthly screeching which I'm sure is the little buggers mating, which makes me jealous as hell, as you can imagine.

I believe it's illegal to hunt foxes but if you ask me, it shouldn't just be legal – it should be compulsory. If only I was in charge...things would be different.

Sunday

Vaping; what's the point? If you want to smoke, smoke and if you don't want to smoke, don't smoke. I would like to smoke, but no-one in this house smokes (although I have my suspicions about the girl), and I don't leave the house, so access to smoking paraphernalia is restricted, to say the least.

Monday

I've been reading back through this journal and it strikes me that some of it is quite depressing. It makes it sound like I'm a miserable bugger, ungrateful for his lot who never does anything but moan. And, of course that's true. But, it's not all true. There are good things about my life and I have resolved to try and be more positive.

So, let me start by saying that my life, though sad and miserable and devoid of true love or any real hope (there I go again), is not unpleasant. I have a roof over my head (permanently), it is warm, I have (too much) food to eat, these people are nice to me, I have my books, my poetry, my television (not my own, but the use of one), the wi-fi works, this journal (obviously), I pay no bills and have no bills to pay, mine is not the mortgage to pay. It never rains on me and I'm not thirsty or hungry – life could be worse.

Tuesday

I don't like pigeons. They are fat and ugly and grey like battleships and they seem too big and out of proportion. Sparrows and robins on the other hand are small and delicate and they dance through the air; they are like butterflies. They are homing pigeons with no home to go to. There are parakeets in the garden – I hear them singing through the wires and talking to each other. They have nothing to say.

I've decided to start using cutlery; I call it 'catlery.' Ha ha. I've seen this lot do it and frankly if they can manage it I don't see why I can't.

I really wish they wouldn't tickle me under my chin; it really is not a nice feeling. They pick me up, these damn children, and stroke me with their little children fingers and flick my ears which they think is funny, but I don't. I purr, and they think I like it. But I don't purr for them, I purr for me. That's my life advice to you: don't purr for others; purr for you. Purring is not that difficult; I'm surprised people can't do it.

I can't find the Sky remote. What is the matter with these people? Why can't they put it back in the right place? I wanted to watch a documentary on Sky Arts and I shall miss it if I can't find the remote. People can be very irritating.

<u>Later</u>

I found the remote. It was down the side of the sofa. I also found a £2 coin, 4 boiled sweets, an ice cream stick, some Sellotape, a love letter, a USB charging cable, 3 socks and a tattered copy of Gabriel Garcia Marques' One Hundred Years of Solitude[58]. I think I know how he feels.

<u>Wednesday</u>

The Bridge series 1 was better than series 2. They're both better than Trapped. The Killing series 1 is better but series 2 is not as good as series 1 of the Bridge. Borgen is not as good as Trapped. Breaking Bad is better than all of them. The Sopranos, there was a series. And The Wire, of course. If you were confined to your house for the rest of your life, I bet you'd watch a lot of TV too[59].

<u>Sunday</u>

What is a cat if I can't trap a bird and kill it for no reason other than my own enjoyment, or chase down an innocent mouse and watch it shrivel in fright and expire before my eyes so that I can extract its offal and leave it bloody and torn on the shiny rug for my owners to find; if I can't creep through the undergrowth swatting at Great Whites and Admirals as they flutter by? What is a cat without a world to wander, a lifetime to live?

I am nothing; a plaything for spoiled children, I am a living ornament, a possession, a conversation piece, a security blanket, a stuffed toy lost in the bedclothes, a cushion, a hot water bottle, a lap dancer. I am all they want me to be but nothing I want to be; if they died or forgot me or passed on I would fade away like the picture on an old TV – I fade to black and am no more.

Tuesday

They went out last night to the theatre. I had the house to myself and baked a cake. They came back late complaining about the weather and nowhere to park and being tired and stressed; do they not realise how hurtful it is to me to hear that; me who can't go out? I am so jealous, how I long for a night out, a party, an event, an invitation, an escape from my prison. It may be a gilded cage – warm and safe and comfortable and well-fed and adored – but it's still a cage. But they'll never understand.

A catalogue was delivered today. I thought it would contain items of interest to cats but, despite the name, it didn't.

Catatonia[60] is a country with a very large cat population. Apparently, most of them don't move much (joke).

Saturday

Laps aren't comfortable. Cats are obviously supposed to enjoy them but believe me, bony knees and shaky thighs and the gap between where your bum sinks down - well, there's better places to fall asleep, believe me. And why do they fidget so and must they insist on watching television while we're trying to rest? Do they think we're deaf? People are strange; I'll never understand humans.

Sunday

Fish is over-rated.

I am bored with my diet. Every day the same dreary packet food – Whiskas, Felix, Whiskas, Felix, Whiskas, Whiskas, Felix, Felix, Whiskas. They think that opening a packet and dumping a load of slimy, slippery, dirty brown slop into a bowl is all they have to do.

Is it too much to ask that they add a bit of style, some panache, some thought into it – at least lay the table, provide some condiments, a napkin, a vase of flowers, even a tea-light? And why always a plastic dish – never some porcelain, the best china, some glass, my own personal dish and not some hand me down cast-off they found in a charity shop which they wipe with a bit of kitchen roll and never clean properly? One of these days I shall expect candles, a table-cloth, soft music, a Hungarian gypsy violinist to serenade me while I eat, a bit of style, not this perfunctory <u>feeding.</u>

I want to dine in and be entertained and pampered; I don't want to be <u>fed.</u>

Monday

The walls are closing in. Not literally you understand, although for all I know maybe the rooms are getting smaller, but I feel trapped here – no, correct that, I <u>am</u> trapped here.

Tuesday

I've never seen Star Wars, read War and Peace, peeled a grape, defaulted on a mortgage, voted Tory, had children, been drunk, taken drugs, sold a pup, cleared the snow from a drive, had a snowball fight, been circumcised, swum underwater, smoked a cigar, broken a promise, sailed a boat, completed a puzzle, understood the point of Cluedo, celebrated Mother's Day, removed a bottle cap with my teeth, had a tattoo (see above), visited Blackpool (or anywhere), broken a plate, split the atom, named a star, seen Back to the Future[61], discovered a planet or calculated Pi[62]. I have never ridden a motor-cycle, made a parachute jump, been in a knife fight, slept with a prostitute, bought a charity record, worn a hat, seen the Taj Mahal, panned for gold, observed a total eclipse, eaten frog's legs, found God, converted to Islam, felt rain on my face or had sex.

I miss not having had sex. I think.

Wednesday

I've made a claim for PPI. I've never had a bank loan but everyone else seems to be claiming and getting money so why shouldn't I? It's like one of those Nigerian email scams – if I make a claim to every bank I can think of there's bound to be one that pays out – just out of guilt. Isn't that what everyone does? I can't believe all these other claims are genuine. The amount the banks have paid out is equivalent to £2000 for every man, woman and child in the country. That seems excessive to me and it doesn't include all the cats like me who've submitted a claim.

We'll see if I'm successful. No begging letters please.

Thursday

I think I'm getting fatter. I caught sight of myself in the mirror earlier and could not believe the fat lump I saw waddling along. I used to be able to lie on my back and roll to the left or right swinging my back legs from side to side – there was no particular reason for it but I could do it so I did – but I tried that just now and lying down I couldn't even see my back legs over the great expanse of furry belly which loomed like a mound of fly-tipping between me and my paws. I think a diet may be in order.

Friday

I was watching this Batman film last night - I think it was called The Dark Knight Rises[63] – good film, although not as good as The Dark Knight[64], which is amazing and one of the best films ever made. And it had this character in it – Catwoman. Catwoman! Not a cat, as you and I might expect, but a person – a woman – dressed as a cat. Now, what's that all about? You ever see a cat dressed as a person? Me neither. But it seems it's acceptable for a woman to dress up like a cat and call herself Catwoman. I tell you, diary, her life seemed a lot different from mine. She wasn't stuck indoors like I am, for one thing, although that could just be in the film, I suppose.

She had a thing with Batman who was played by Christian Bale, who was okay – Catwoman was played by Anne Hathaway, not my favourite actress, although when she sang that Susan Boyle song[65] in Les Misérables, it positively made the fur on the back of my neck stand up.

Apparently, there was a whole Catwoman[66] film which starred Halle Berry, but IMDB doesn't rate it, so I won't bother.

<u>Saturday</u>

I have started to drink wine in the afternoons. It started like this. I was bored, everyone was out. I was rooting around in the kitchen (as you do) and I knocked over a bottle of wine which had been left open. It didn't smash but the wine leaked on the floor and I thought I'd better clear it up, so I started licking. Such joy, such excitement, such taste overwhelmed me. I finished it all and lay down by the back door with the sun streaming in and I lay there, fuzzy and drowsy and woozy with my head spinning but so blissfully relaxed and chilled out like I had not known before.

Since that slight beginning I have sought out more wines and I think they may suspect something. After all, there are only so many bottles of wine that a cat can accidentally knock over before it starts to look suspicious and I think they may be on to me. I had a Prosecco which I thought over-rated if I'm honest, but a delicate red at just the right temperature is like a blood boost and it warms your bones and my troubles slip away from me.

Sunday

Unrequited love is the least of love.

What if this is all there is? That I should play out my short life in this tumbledown house in some Godforsaken suburb, miles away from my friends and family (whoever they are – I never knew my father), forced to prowl these lonely corridors with only my notebook and pencil for company. Never to feel the wind on my face and the sun in my eyes, never to lie on cool sand by an azure sea, or tramp the high mountain passes through depthless snow, never to trudge through the leaves and lianas of an Amazon rainforest, the cackle of monkeys and macaws ringing in my ears?

Is it really possible that my sad scribbles will never see the light of day, never grace the dizzy heights of the Amazon best-seller charts?

Oh well. I wonder what's for dinner?

Later

Oh, West Wickham what have you done?

Oh, West Wickham, what have you become?

No-one famous lived there, no-one famous came from there, no-one famous will die there. You are anonymous and empty and forgotten, but you are home and you are mine. All the broken sadnesses of my empty, pointless life come back to haunt me.

West Wickham, I sing my song for you.

West Wickham, I recite my poem for you.

West Wickham, may I cry for you.

West Wickham, may I die for you.

You are my story, my soul, my world, my universe.

West Wickham, you are mine. I love you.

It's the hope that kills you. It's the hope that kills you. The hope, the hope, the hope, the hope, the hope, the hope, the hope, the…

Lose your dreams and you might lose your mind.

I've lost my dreams.

<u>Monday</u>

Wow! I just read yesterday's entry back and boy, I must have been having a bad day! Maybe, I was depressed, or drunk, or the food was off, or there wasn't enough of it (unlikely) or maybe it's just a bit of SAD – Seasonal Affective Disorder. I read somewhere that during the dark months, people (and I assume that includes cats) can feel a bit down because of the lack of sunlight.

Now, I don't know why that should affect me as I've never been outside, so I don't actually know what sunlight feels like, but that doesn't mean I can't get it – SAD, I mean.

Anyway, whatever it was, I've cheered up a bit now and I'll tell you why – we're on the move!

Yep, it's house-moving time. I don't know what it will mean for me – I expect the inside of one house looks much like another, but I'll be able to find some new places to sleep and some new areas to hide in, and I won't miss that damn ghost and my tunnel which I never went back to. I'll miss my pussy hole though; I liked that. But who knows? Maybe I'll find another.

And I've decided to finish with you diary and move on to a new chapter in my life by closing this chapter of my life. I'm going to leave the diary here – maybe another cat will find it and learn about me.

Byeeeee!

Epilogue

The journal ends here. We do not know what happened to Sir Ian or whether that was even his name. Sometimes we sense his presence – on the stairs, sprawled on the rug in front of the fire, stretched out on the carpet warming himself by the radiator, sitting by the back door drinking his wine and dreaming of the open air, snuggled down on the bed with the other stuffed animals, sleeping in his pussy hole (which we never found), in the cupboard under the stairs furiously and vainly digging his tunnel. (The scratch marks are still there; one of these days we must get them repaired).

We did not know him but reading the journal we feel we knew him and we miss him. He has taught us something about his life and the lives of others and of how we should treat our pets.

We too have a cat now. We have called him Sir Ian, in memory of our unknown friend. We used to keep him inside, but we don't any more. We have installed a cat flap and Sir Ian spends a lot of time in the garden, chasing birds and playing with the other local cats. He seems to have made friends with the cat from next door. She is a soft-haired Birman called Fluffy. We think that maybe they're in love.

Notes

---

[1] 'Sir Ian' is a reference to Sir Ian McKellen, who appears in the second series of 'Extras,' written, directed and starring Ricky Gervais and Stephen Merchant.

[2] 'Larry' is the name of the Downing Street cat.

[3] Cfer as in c for cat.

[4] Sir Ian is having a little joke. 'Property is Theft' was coined by Joseph Proudhon, a forerunner of Karl Marx, in his 1840 book: What is Property? Groucho Marx was an American comic actor, very popular in the 1930s; his notable (and very funny) films, in which he starred with his brothers Harpo and Chico, include A Night at the Opera, A Day at the Races and Duck Soup.

[5] Guantanamo Bay in Cuba is American territory and is used by the Americans as a prison camp for suspected terrorists. It is not subject to American judicial processes and a number of people thought to be members of Al Qaeda or other terrorist groups, have been held there indefinitely, without being charged with any crime.

[6] Franz Kafka, Czech author of the early 20th century. He is best known for The Trial, about a man who is tried and convicted of a crime, but who never finds out what he is actually being accused of, and Metamorphosis, about a man who wakes up one morning and finds he has been turned into a cockroach.

[7] In August 2012, Julian Assange, Australian founder of Wikileaks, sought refuge in the Ecuadorean Embassy in London. He was in London and sought to avoid extradition to Sweden, where he was

wanted for questioning on sexual assault charges. He claimed that if he went to Sweden, he would be extradited to the USA to face charges. In May 2017, the Swedish authorities announced that they were dropping their investigation. As of this date (July 2018), Assange remains in the Embassy; concerned that if he left he would be arrested by British police to face charges of breaching his bail conditions and of wasting everyone's time.

[8] The extravagantly coiffed, serial philanderer, opportunist, Brexiteer and lying journalist - Boris Johnson - was a British politician. He served as Lord Mayor of London from 2008 to 2016 and as Foreign Secretary in Theresa May's Conservative government from 2016 to 2018, before resigning in June 2018, after failing to get his own way. At the time of writing (July 2018), he is busy forging a new path in the political wilderness, still trying to convince people he was right about Brexit.

[9] This is a pun on The World According to Garp, a 1979 novel by the American writer John Irving.

[10] This is a pun on Catch 22, the first novel by the American writer, Joseph Heller. Published in 1961, it is a story about American airmen, based in Italy during the Second Wold War; it is one of the finest, blackly comic novels of war ever written.

[11] This is a pun on One Hundred Years of Solitude, published in 1967 by the Columbian writer and winner of the 1982 Nobel prize for literature, Gabriel Garcia Marquez. Marquez wrote a number of other highly regarded novels and died in 2014.

[12] This is a pun on Cider with Rosie, an autobiographical work first published in 1959 by the British writer, Laurie Lee.

[13] The Shawshank Redemption is a 1974 film directed by Frank Darabont, from a story by Stephen King and starring Morgan Freeman and Tim Robbins, which is not nearly as good as everyone seems to think. But it's all right. It is very long and is shown on British television at least once in every 24-hour period as a way of filling up the schedules.

[14] Batman was the first in a string of films about the black-clad hero. Released in 1989 and directed by Tim Burton, it starred Michael Keaton as the caped crusader and Jack Nicholson as his nemesis and greatest opponent – The Joker.

[15] The first Superman film ('you'll believe a man can fly'), released in 1978 and directed by Richard Donner, starred Margot Kidder, Gene Hackman and Christopher Reeve as the superhero who could fly. In a supreme ironic twist, Reeve was later paralysed from the neck down after being thrown from a horse. He died in 2004.

[16] Sir Ian is referencing F Scott Fitzgerald's 1920s masterpiece, The Great Gatsby.

[17] As above, Moby Dick.

[18] 50 Shades of Grey was a very popular erotic fantasy novel of supreme artistic merit, written by E L James. It was later made into a film, directed by Sam Taylor-Johnson. James has written a number of sequels, most of which feature variations on the word Grey.

[19] The haunting and mysterious song Ruby Tuesday, written by Keith Richards of the Rolling Stones, was a big hit for Melanie (Safka) in 1971.

[20] Sir Ian is attempting to copy James Joyce's writing style in his masterpiece Ulysses: he doesn't really succeed.

[21] Create and Craft is a TV channel which sells card-stock, ribbon, glue and other rubbish, to enable people to make greetings cards with which to stave off terminal boredom and annoy their friends.

[22] The Count of Monte Cristo was a novel by the French writer Alexander Dumas.

[23] The Man in the Iron Mask was a novel by the French writer Alexander Dumas, about a man incarcerated who was forced to wear an iron mask, so that his identity was unknown.

[24] 2001: A Space Odyssey was written by Arthur C Clarke and directed by Stanley Kubrick. It was first released in 1968 and remains popular with hippies and geeks to this day. Parts of it are brilliant, but as Sir Ian rather perceptibly observes, there are sections which are incomprehensible and pretentious beyond belief. As a minor footnote, Leonard Rossiter from TV's Rising Damp and the Campari adverts, plays a Russian doctor. The music, however, by Strauss and others, is supremely well-chosen.

[25] 'Daisy, Daisy, give me your answer do/ I'm half-crazy over my love for you/ it won't be a stylish marriage/ I can't afford a carriage/But you'll look sweet/ upon the seat/of a bicycle made for two.

[26] The Great Escape, directed by John Sturges in 1963, starred Richard Attenborough, Steve McQueen, James Coburn, Donald Pleasance, James Garner, Charles Bronson and a host of other great actors. It is a superb film and told the true story of a daring escape from a German prisoner-of-war camp by means of a tunnel which the prisoners painstakingly dug beneath the perimeter fence. Although some 76 prisoners escaped through the tunnel, 50 were captured and shot by the SS; a shocking war crime. Only 3 of the escapees actually made it to safety.

[27] Steve McQueen's character – Hilts 'the Cooler King' - unlike most of the others, was not based on a real person. He was included in the film as the producers wanted a big American star to appear. He escaped through the tunnel but was captured by the Germans while attempting to jump a fence on a motor-bike. Unlike the luckless Brits, he was not shot but was returned to the camp.

[28] The Musgrave Ritual by Sir Arthur Conan Doyle appears in The Memoirs of Sherlock Homes and is one of Doyle's finest Holmes stories. In the story, a wicked butler is interred in a vault by those he has wronged – his remains discovered later by Sherlock Holmes and his faithful side-kick, Dr Watson.

[29] Anthem, written by Leonard Cohen, from the album The Future, released in 1992.

[30] 'Catolics' – Sir Ian is setting up an elaborate pun. He is, of course, referring to Catholics, a persecuted minority under Cromwell during the 17th century. Many Catholics were forced to worship in secret and built 'Priest's Holes' in their homes – secret, hidden

passage-ways and rooms where the visiting priest could hide if the house was searched by Cromwell's men.

[31] Sir Ian is referring to the widely-held belief that someone infected with rabies is scared of water. It is not known whether cats with rabies are similarly affected, although Sir Ian clearly believes that they are.

[32] Some Like it Hot was a 1959 film directed by Billy Wilder, starring Tony Curtis and Jack Lemmon as a couple of musicians in 1920s Chicago who accidentally witness the St Valentine's Day massacre. In order to escape from Al Capone's gangsters, they dress as women and escape to Miami, where they meet, and Tony Curtis's character falls in love with, Sugar Kowalski, played by a radiant Marilyn Monroe. It is a wonderful film and possibly Monroe's finest performance.

[33] Mormons follow the religion of Mormonism, founded by Joseph Smith in New York in the 1820s. Known as the Church of Jesus Christ of Latter Day Saints, it is based on Christianity but includes a number of variations which Smith claimed to have discovered in the Book of Mormon; Mormons do not believe in monogamy – hence Sir Ian's little joke. Henry VIII was not a Mormon. The Book of Mormon is also the title of a hilarious musical which satirises the Mormons and their evangelical tendencies.

[34] Scientology is an absurd and bizarre belief system, developed by the American Science Fiction writer L Ron Hubbard as a way of becoming rich. It has a number of adherents, including those mentioned by Sir Ian.

[35] Euclid, an Ancient Greek, flourished 300 BC, is regarded as the father of geometry.

[36] Pythagoras was an Ancient Greek mathematician, best known for his 'theorem' – the squares of the triangle are equal to the squares on the other 2 sides, or something.

[37] The Man who was Thursday by GK Chesterton, concerns a group of criminals who, as a disguise, name themselves after the days of the week.

[38] The Cat as Big as the Ritz. Sir Ian is indulging in another of his cat puns. He is referring to F Scott Fitzgerald's short story The Diamond as Big as the Ritz.

[39] The Cat and the Canary was a 1939 film starring Bob Hope and Paulette Goddard. Sir Ian is making another of his jokes - Hope plays a character called Wally Campbell; he does not play a canary.

[40] Cheryl Cole rose to fame after appearing on Pop Idol and becoming part of the band Girls Aloud. She subsequently appeared on a number of occasions as a judge on the X Factor. Unlucky in relationships, she has been married three times, first (and most famously) to the footballer, Ashley Cole.

[41] John Paul Getty III was kidnapped at the age of 17 by Italian gangsters. His famous grandfather – J Paul Getty, the richest man in the world – initially refused to pay a ransom, as a result of which the gangsters cut off one of Getty's ears. The story was made into a film in 2017 and was notable for the fact that old man Getty was originally played by Kevin Spacey. After Spacey was accused of a series of sexual assaults, the director Ridley Scott made the

decision to re-shoot all of his scenes with Christopher Plummer in the Spacey role; Plummer was best known for his role in The Sound of Music. Apart from this minor snippet, the film has nothing to recommend it.

[42] Sir Ian is making a reference to Wichita Lineman, that fabulous love song written by Jimmy Webb and performed by Glen Campbell: 'I am a lineman for the county/And I drive the main road/Searchin' in the sun for another overload/I hear you singin' in the wire/I can hear you through the whine/And the Wichita Lineman is still on the line.'

[43] Watchtower is the magazine of the Jehovah's Witnesses.

[44] Betterware is a catalogue containing homewares and cleaning products, delivered to people's homes.

[45] Sir Ian is quoting TE Lawrence (1888 – 1935), better known as Lawrence of Arabia: *'All men dream; but not equally. Those who dream by night in the dusty recesses of their minds wake up in the day to find it was vanity, but the dreamers of the day are dangerous men, for they may act their dreams with open eyes, to make it possible.'* Lawrence was a British Army Colonel who was instrumental in supporting Prince Feisal, leader of the Arab Revolt against the Ottoman Turks during the First World War. Lawrence subsequently wrote an account of the conflict and his role in it – The Seven Pillars of Wisdom. He was killed in 1935 in a motorcycle accident in Dorset. A film about him – Lawrence of Arabia – was made in 1962; directed by David Lean, it starred Peter O'Toole as

Lawrence and Alec Guinness as Prince Feisal. As an interesting, albeit minor footnote, the film – although 3.5 hours long - does not contain a single female speaking role.

[46] Sir Ian is showing off again: Marcel Proust (1871 - 1922): A La Recherche du Temps Perdu, James Joyce (1882 - 1941): Finnegan's Wake, Thomas Pynchon (b 1937): Gravity's Rainbow, Vladimir Nabokov (1899 - 1977): Lolita, Charles Dickens (1812 - 1870): Great Expectations, Oliver Twist and The Pickwick Papers, John Steinbeck (1902 – 1968, winner of the Nobel Prize for Literature in 1962): The Grapes of Wrath, Julian Barnes (b 1946): The Sense of an Ending, Ian McEwan (b 1948): Atonement, Leo Tolstoy (1828 - 1910): War and Peace and Anna Karenina, Fyodor Dostoyevsky (1821 - 1881): Crime and Punishment, The Brothers Karamazov, The Idiot.

[47] The Godfather part II, the sequel (and prequel) to the original Godfather film, was directed by Francis Ford Coppola and released in 1974. It starred Al Pacino as Michael Corleone with Diane Keaton playing his soon to be estranged wife, and Robert de Niro playing the role of the young Don Corleone, who was played in the first film by Marlon Brando. It is one of the finest films ever made and possibly the only time that a sequel has eclipsed the original.

[48] The Third Man is widely regarded as one of the finest films ever made. Released in 1949, from a script by Graham Greene, it was filmed and set in Vienna, immediately after the last war. It starred Orson Welles as Harry Lime - the mysterious 'third man' - and Joseph Cotten as Holly Martins, an old friend who comes to Vienna to find him. Alida Valli plays Welles' girl-friend Anna Schmidt and, after Welles' death, Cotten harbours dreams that she will fall in

love with him, with the brutal consequences that Sir Ian alludes to. The film is also remembered for its haunting theme music, played on the zither by Anton Karras and which, coincidentally, I now have as the ring-tone on my iPhone.

[49] Three Days by Lucinda Williams, from the album World Without Tears, released in 2003.

[50] Alexander the Great – 356 BC to 323 BC - is reputed to have wept when he was told that there were no more worlds to conquer.

[51] Cat Ballou was a 1965 Western which starred Jane Fonda and Lee Marvin.

[52] Cat on a Hot Tin Roof is a play by Tennessee Williams; it won Williams the Pulitzer Prize for Drama in 1955. It was made into a film in 1958 starring Elizabeth Taylor and Paul Newman.

[53] Pavlov's Dog was an American band of the 1970s. They released 2 early good albums – At the Sound of the Bell (1975) and Pampered Menial (1976), before largely disappearing from view. Their songs featured the strange, haunting voice of David Surkamp.

[54] Sir Ian probably means Babel, their break-through album, released in 2012.

[55] TS Eliot's collection of cat poems – Old Possum's Book of Practical Cats - was published in 1939 and in 1981 was made into a hugely successful musical – Cats - by the composer Andrew Lloyd Webber.

[56] Sir Ian is probably referring to a Maine Coon – a large, long-haired, curiously popular breed of cats; although it is not clear why he regards them as 'posh.'

[57] The 'Danish woman' as Sir Ian rather dismisses her as, is Sandi Toksvig, the well-known comedian, writer and television presenter. She took over from the sainted Stephen Fry as the presenter of QI in October 2016.

[58] See footnote 11 above.

[59] The Bridge was a Swedish/Danish crime drama which debuted on British television in 2012 and ran for 4 series. It starred Sofia Helin as Saga Noren, a Swedish detective. The Wire was an American crime drama devised by David Simon, which ran for five series starting in 2002. It is the programme that brought fame to Idris Elba, who played the drug dealer and enforcer, Stringer Bell. Trapped was a crime drama set in Iceland. Borgen was a Danish political drama which ran for 3 series starting in 2010 and starred Sidse Babett Knudsen as the Danish Prime Minister. Devised by Vince Gilligan, Breaking Bad was a drama about a high school teacher, played by Bryan Cranston, in New Mexico who is diagnosed with cancer and decides to become a manufacturer and dealer in crystal meth, in order to raise money for his family. It started in 2008 and ran for 5 series. The Sopranos, devised by David Chase, ran for 6 series and 86 episodes starting in 1999 and starred the late James Gandolfini as Tony Soprano.

[60] Sir Ian is guilty of more puns. There is no such country as Catatonia. Catatonia is a mental condition in which a person appears to freeze and go into a sort of trance.

[61] Back to the Future – hugely popular film, released in 1985, directed by Robert Zemeckis and starring Christopher Lloyd and Michael J Fox as teenager Marty McFly. The film featured a DeLorean car, a futuristic (at the time) gull-winged sports car designed by the American John DeLorean and built in Belfast, on the back of huge subsidies offered by the British government. DeLorean's company went bankrupt shortly afterwards, taking most of the Government's money down with it, but his car lives on in this dreary film.

[62] Pi is 22 divided by 7, a sum that ultimately produces an infinite number; it is usually shortened to 3.14.

[63] The Dark Knight Rises – released in 2012, directed by Christopher Nolan, starred Christian Bale as Batman and Anne Hathaway as Catwoman.

[64] The Dark Knight – released in 2008, directed by Christopher Nolan, starred Christian Bale as Batman and the late Heath Ledger as The Joker.

[65] 'Susan Boyle song' – Sir Ian is having a little joke. The song he refers to is I' Dreamed a Dream' which appears in the stage show and also the film of Les Misérables where it is sung by Anne Hathaway. The singer Susan Boyle covered the song in her original Britain's Got Talent audition in 2009 and brought the house down.

[66] Catwoman – released in 2004, directed by Pitof, starred Halle Berry as Catwoman.

23516159R00073

Printed in Great Britain
by Amazon